Anders Tunek is a Swede living halftime in Sweden and halftime in Sri Lanka. He is married to a Sri Lankan. Previously, Tunek lived also in Portugal and in Germany. He made a professional career in the pharmaceutical industry but took early retirement because he wanted to live a different life. Among other things he wanted to pursue his passions, one of which is writing fiction.

THE SISTERS

Anders Tunek

THE SISTERS

Vanguard Press

A CIP catalogue record for this title is
available from the British Library.

ISBN 978 1 80016 639 4

*Vanguard Press is an imprint of
Pegasus Elliot Mackenzie Publishers Ltd.*
www.pegasuspublishers.com

First Published in 2023

**Vanguard Press
Sheraton House Castle Park
Cambridge England**

Printed & Bound in Great Britain

To Saku, Elvira, Jonas, and Kim.

To my beloved wife Saku whose sensuality always inspires me, and for how she believes in and patiently encourages my ambitions. Thank you, dear, for also sharing with me the richness of the English language.

1

Sakuntala and I sat in the pleasant Tea Lounge at the Cinnamon Grand Hotel in Colombo, Sri Lanka. Saku had ordered a lime soda, and a waiter was busy making my Irish Coffee on a trolley in front of us. Earlier in the evening we had enjoyed a typical Sri Lankan dinner with curries and string hoppers. As usual, in the presence of Saku, I felt an attraction difficult to control. I wanted to grab one of her thighs with both hands, lean over her and kiss her. Such a behaviour is not part of this culture. Saku is always perfectly aware of my state of emotion. She enjoyed my excitement, something I could see in the way her asymmetric lips were shaped. This night she had a simple, long, western dress exposing most tastefully her wonderful ankles and lower parts of her calves. She stretched her beautiful legs in a way she knew made me almost painfully aroused. She knows me so well.

At about eleven we cleared the bill with a generous tip. We strolled through the nicely cooled lounge and exited at the main entrance out into the evening heat of around 30°C. Down on Galle Road we stopped a tuk-tuk and ten minutes later we were in Saku's apartment.

2

"Hi Anders! I don't know where on this planet you are, but I thought the following might be of interest: Remains of a man have been found buried in the peat bog located between Östrahult and Hällerum, 15 kilometres southeast of Vimmerby. An area most dear and well-known to you if my memory serves me well. It is a brutal murder. I will give details when we talk. First it was thought the body had been lying there for many centuries. However, now we estimate the murder was committed 70 – 80 years ago, between 1935 and 1945. Thus, you probably walked right over him as a child already when he was rather newly buried, and much more recently as well. I know these are among your favourite walking areas. We should try to investigate this although the killer has walked free. Retroactive justice. I appoint you as Principal Investigator for the case. Forensic and all sorts of analyses are ongoing. I look forward to hearing from you. Your friend and boss Jan N."

I was astonished and dismayed to read the email which I opened only late morning after a tender night and a pleasant awakening. My most beloved places on earth indeed, to which I return whenever I have the opportunity. It is not possible for me to think about these areas without returning to the childhood dialect in my thoughts. For some reason, we always called this peat bog the 'Wild Moss'. Not at all far away, 1½ kilometres maximally, from my childhood home, yet one feels as in another world out there. When I took partial retirement at 55, I transferred ownership of my two-room apartment in Stockholm to my kids, and instead bought back my childhood home some 300 kilometres south of the capital. This is one of the most sparsely populated regions of the southern part of Sweden. Simply wonderful areas, far away from all metropoles, not much exploited by tourism. Saku and I now have my childhood home as our Swedish paradise, and we spend money and effort to renovate the house. As Jan Norberg correctly assumes, we walk out in the Wild Moss quite often. In all likelihood over the grave, or at least in the close proximity to it. If it is a grave. It is probably rather a dump, or a very secure place to hide away something unpleasant. The probability of something ever being unearthed out there must be as close to zero as it can get.

The first times I walked through the Wild Moss must have been in the mid-1950s, when I was between 5 and 10 years old. Then always with my father, and he always with a shotgun over his shoulder. Usually, we came home with one or two hares, and I remember once I proudly could show a big, pitch black, capercaillie to my little sisters. Later I built hideaways out there to study and film capercaillie cocks courting hens in March-April with snow still covering the ground. Few, if any, now living persons know the area better than I, but even I can get lost on a cloudy day if I'm out there without a compass. Large areas are covered by densely grown, short, twisted pines and birches, and other parts of the bog by knee-high shrubs of different species. Here and there an old, robust pine with a few branches only near the top. Many times, one can see no more than two metres to any side due to the dense vegetation, and the ground is marshy. Walking in the area is demanding since all the time there is the risk of sinking down to your knees and sometimes deeper. Monotonous but also a feeling of magic. In cold winters rich with snow, parts of the area are wonderful for cross-country skiing. During the first four decades of the twentieth century peat moss was extracted from here in a small industrial scale.

Saku saw I was shaken and overtaken by emotions.

"Dear! Have you read something unpleasant?"

"Yes. That is the least one can say. It has been discovered that a murder was committed close to my home just about five to ten years before I was born. You and I have been right on the site picking cloudberries."

I translated the email from Jan.

"Oh! So, you will have to go to Sweden right away I suppose?"

"Most likely. I must call Jan."

"May I join you in two-three weeks? I have some matters to sort out first."

"I will long for you. But you may not understand fully what the weather is like up there this time of the year. Mid-February. It's winter in Scandinavia."

"The weather is irrelevant if one is so much in love as I am. Apart from that, as you know I love cool and even cold weather."

"You will have an overdose of coolness. However, this year, so far, it is unusually mild. No snow and no ground frost. Yet cold for a tropical flower. Indoors the opposite. We will light a fire in the tiled stove in the bedroom. We will both be so hot we will get burnt when we touch."

"I know, my love. And I know how to get you there even without the stove."

I had started to work as a police officer in Stockholm aged 25. I moved around in the country and steadily rose in the hierarchy, educated myself, until appointed Chief Investigator at the Central Criminal Police Unit in Stockholm at age 39, which was considered early for reaching such a position. As Chief Criminal Investigator I have been extraordinarily successful. I know very well I am considered, both by colleagues and by the public, as one of the best in the country. With patience, endurance, analytical sharpness, humility, high level of education in many areas, I have solved many high-profile cases, and I can conduct myself in almost any social circumstance. Thanks to a small heritage, wise living and saving, and overall positive economic developments in the country, I had the resources to take partial retirement already at 55. I wanted to live parts of the rest of my life as a somewhat luxurious backpacker. Seeing the world on my own. A rucksack on my back but staying mostly at reasonably comfortable hotels. Things changed. During a one-week stop-over in Sri Lanka four years earlier, on my way back home to Sweden from Tonga, through a miraculous coincidence, I met Saku. My life was turned upside down. At that time, I was 60 and Saku 56.

Jan Norberg had been my colleague and he was my lifelong particularly good friend. He never was a fantastic investigator, but an excellent organiser and a most sympathetic and nice guy. Jan was also intelligent, and astute in identifying his shortcomings and strengths. He had climbed the ladder, and now he was my boss. He created a positive atmosphere, and he distributed the resources well. It was now 9.30 a.m. Scandinavian time. I dialled Jan's number on Skype, and he took the call on the first signal.

"Hi old man! What were you up to down there in the deep forests in the good old days? By the way, where are you? When talking to you one never knows if you sit in a bar down here on the corner, or if you are on the opposite side of the globe."

"I'm far away. In the warmth and heat of Sri Lanka. I hope even a narrowminded guy like you understands the meteorological as well as the erotic undercurrent of my words. So, what have you found?"

"I have not been down there in the peat bog to see for myself. As you know I'm most comfortable sitting on my chair in my office. Those who have seen it say it is dreadful. The skull is cut nearly into two parts, and it seems he has been given a blow on the neck also. A vertebra high up is gravely wounded. The tool could have been a sharp axe or something similar."

"Hm! How was he placed? And how was he discovered?"

"In the peat bog about half a metre under the surface. A hunter and part-time farmer, who recently moved down to the wilderness from Stockholm, had come up with the crazy idea to grow some sort of cabbage as fodder for moose out there. He was digging a hole to see what the soil was like. He got a shock when the spade hit a foot. The foot had a sock on but no shoe. The man called the police in Vimmerby who in turn informed Forensic Medicine in Linköping. Both forensic as well as archaeological expertise were sent. On the day before yesterday came a preliminary estimate of how long he had been lying there, and only yesterday they discovered the macabre physical violence that had been exerted. The archaeologists could relax and go home. It is something for the police."

"Yes, we should try to find out who he is, if at all possible. Show some sort of retroactive respect. What happens out there right now?"

"Two investigators from Kalmar are on site with two helpers to dig further. I will send to you the mobile number to officer Jan Bengtsson. So far, they have found he wore socks, jersey, linen shirt, underwear, and trousers. All clothing fairly well preserved. The Central Criminal Police unit should take over, and I appoint you as Principal Investigator. No one knows the area and its history like you. The guys are digging and uncovering the corpse so that it can be transported up to Forensic Medicine in Linköping within a few days."

"Jan, I have understood. Thanks for the confidence. I will come to the site as soon as practically possible. Probably I will be on a plane on the day after tomorrow. That peaceful place! My mother, she was born 1926, grew up on a farm not much more than one kilometre away from this site. My grandfather and his helpers may have harvested oats just a few hundred metres away as they buried the body! How ghastly!"

Early next morning I received another message from Jan Norberg:

"It's getting worse. They have found another one. Half a metre from the first. A woman. Similar, if not identical, physical impact on head and neck."

I spoke to officer Jan Bengtsson a couple of times as they were digging and sweating out on the bog. He couldn't tell much more than I knew already. The woman had been a victim of a similar gruesome violence as the man. The bodies were nearly ready to be transported up to Forensic Medicine at the University Hospital Linköping. All sorts of experts had been out there in the wilderness without being able to draw conclusions other than the obvious. Now was the time for more comprehensive genetic and chemical analyses.

3

Saku insisted on coming with me to the airport. No one could be more passionately in love than she. Her head rested on my shoulder, and my hand rested on her knee. We stayed away from kisses out of respect for Saku's driver Ravi. It took time to get out of central Colombo since we were forced to travel during rush hour, but once on the highway we were at the airport within 20 minutes.

"I'll come to you as soon as I can. Take care my love! Be safe."

"Don't forget the spices. I want you and your curries. I will keep the house warm."

SriLanka to Doha, Qatar to Copenhagen. High-speed train to Nässjö and bus to Vimmerby, a small town of about 10000 souls. Then taxi the 13 kilometres through the woods to my house in Hällerum. In its heydays Hällerum counted 38 inhabitants, now a few less than that live here permanently. The weather was pleasant for February. It felt like springtime already. Dry and sunny. However, after two months in Sri Lanka, my sense for heat and chill had been readjusted, thus I shivered whatever I put on. I entered my house, about 1½ kilometre from the peat bog where the bodies had been found, five days after receiving the first message from Jan Norberg.

My brother-in-law had put on the heating in the house and refuelled the car. My car was a 28-year-old Volvo 245 which I had owned for 17 years without one single problem, except that it consumed 1.2 litres per 10 kilometres. It is of course irresponsible to pollute the environment with a vehicle like this, so any day soon I must buy a new car. The first I did after unpacking was to visit my mum in the assisted living home in the little village Tuna, five kilometres from my house. She was 90, always in a good mood, and she had knife-sharp memories of many events from her childhood, while what happened yesterday was more in a haze. I was too jet-lagged to initiate a conversation about her recollections of persons working out in the Wild Moss when she was a child. That would have to wait a few days, until my own thoughts were organised and clear. Instead, we talked about this and that. Mama was very interested in 'my new wife', however, she had difficulty in remembering Saku's name and nationality. Saku had become very fond of my mum. The positive feelings were reciprocal, and Mama spoke to Saku without being concerned that Saku at first did not understand a word.

After a cup of coffee with Mama, I shopped at the local grocery store in Tuna, drove to the house to unload, and then to Vimmerby to the liquor store to buy a couple of bottles of wine, then to the grocery supermarket to get a few special items they did not offer at the local store in Tuna, and finally, I picked up a pizza at my favourite pizzeria. Back home I enjoyed the pizza, a glass of wine, and the warmth in front of the tiled stove. I started the WIFI and read a few WhatsApp messages from Saku. So loving and caring. I rang her up, and she enjoyed and encouraged my transformation to a butterfly. Later in the evening, at seven, I called officer Jan Bengtsson.

"Hello Jan, this is Anders Andersson. Finally, I have landed in my house in Hällerum. How are you? Where are you?"

"Hi Anders! Welcome! Nice up here in Scandinavia also, isn't it? Feels like spring. We eat and drink and have a good time at the Town Hotel in Vimmerby."

"I thought so. Enjoy yourselves. Can we meet out on the peat bog tomorrow?"

"Certainly. The bodies, however, are at Forensic Medicine in Linköping since the day before yesterday. I guess you want to meet at the site anyway. I'm sure you know where the old railway was running through the area. Along the remains of the railway there are several hunting towers, and these towers are numbered. Can we meet at hunting tower number eleven at nine o'clock? Is that OK? From that point onwards we have marked with plastic ribbon strips. Without the strips we would never find our way neither in nor out of the bog. Our plans are to finish off tomorrow and then go back home. I don't see what more we can do. You might have something to suggest. By the way, yesterday we bumped into three moose. We heard a loud crack, and then saw the backs of them slowly walking away from us."

"The Railway. I will find my way out there with my eyes covered. We locals still simply say, 'The Railway', despite the fact that the last train travelled there 31st of August 1958. There are always moose out there. Perhaps the densest moose population in the country. I have been in the area hundreds, probably thousands of times, and most certainly I must have trampled the dead bodies many times. Now I'll have another glass of red. I recommend Portuguese wines: Douro, Dao, Alentejo, Setubal and so many others. Undeservedly forgotten up here beside all other wines."

4

At 8.15 next morning I arrived at a crossroad about a hundred metres from hunting tower eleven. I had walked the 1½ kilometres from my home through the sawmill and into the forest, mostly on The Railway. The rails were removed 1959 when I was 9 years of age, but long stretches of the causeway have since been retained and maintained as a narrow road perfectly driveable for normal vehicles, tractors, and even small lorries. The railway, built 1900–1905, penetrated straight as a pin through the wilderness, the straight sections interrupted only by drawn-out bends. Rocks had been blown up to pave the way for the rails, thus on some stretches the trains had travelled in narrow, though not very deep, canyons. The road that now remains almost 60 years after the rails were removed is much better than many other roads in the area. Straight, even, and without sharp ups and downs.

Out here one has a physical sense of the freshness of the air. Smell of conifers. Usually, a soft sound from gentle winds touching the tops of the trees. However, on this day, there was no wind whatsoever. Distant sounds from the sawmill, but the moos of cows have largely gone silent. The small-scale dairy and agricultural production that, for example, my grandparents had as their livelihood is not sufficiently profitable today. Moose, deer, hare and capercaillie roam around here more than ever. This is far away from any metropolitan centres. A few Germans and Dutch of the type who seek calm and tranquillity come here, but Swedes are largely absent. They prefer to sit at home watching TV, playing computer games, and surfing the internet.

This crossroad where I now stood was where another small road diverted from The Railway and led up to the remains of a small house about 100 metres from The Railway. Today only the foundation stones are left of the house that once was home to people. Still there is a root cellar, nearly intact, albeit a bit filthy. Just a new door, a thorough cleaning, and the cellar could probably be used today. During the moose hunt in October, we light a fire at the entrance of the root cellar and grill sausages, sitting in a semicircle in front of the cellar. Wanderers are reminded by a brass plate, erected by the local community association, that the name of this settlement was Kirsta. It was located just at the edge of the Wild Moss, and here had lived the people who tried to make a business out of these meagre natural resources. The peat moss was dug up, soaking wet and heavy, dried in the sun, and pulled out to the railway for further transportation to customers.

This continued till the late 1930s or early 1940s. Today Kirsta is surrounded by complete wilderness. I estimated the site where the bodies were found to be about 600 metres away. I had clear memories of an old man called Nisse, long gone, who came to my home almost every evening during my childhood in the early and mid-1950s to collect the previous day's newspaper. I remember Mama once told me that Nisse, as a younger man, had been one of those living and working out in Kirsta.

People living in Kirsta had not necessarily been involved in, or were not necessarily victims of, the killings. Still, somehow, it feels that's where I should start digging, if I should dig into this ugly crime at all. The Kirsta inhabitants were in their active ages when the murders were committed, and they worked out here. Each day, with few exceptions, they were in the immediate vicinity to where the graves were dug. Utterly few others, even in those days, had any knowledge of the area.

I stood in deep thought at the remains of Kirsta, when I heard a vehicle coming and halting down on The Railway. Two minutes later I was at the crossing and greeted Jan Bengtsson.

"Hi. I'm Anders Andersson. Nice to meet you."

"Good morning. I'm Jan Bengtsson. It's an honour meeting you. You are renowned, and we are proud you have your roots in this county. May I introduce my colleague Sven Lindgren also from the Kalmar Police. We have been here for more than a week. Others who have worked here left this morning. For a few days there were six of us digging."

"Hi Sven. Yes, you have found something indeed. One wonders what could have led to such a heinous crime out here in the middle of nowhere."

"Yes. One dares not even try to imagine what it must have been like when it happened. Horrible."

We walked slowly the 100 metres on The Railway to hunting tower eleven, and from there straight into the bog. After five minutes Sven, who otherwise was a man of few words, said:

"It was just here we saw the moose yesterday. You know what; I have never seen a wild moose before. I did not see much of them now either, but it was just such an experience to see them as shadows moving away from us."

I felt that these guys, particularly Sven, needed some education:

"There are always moose out here, but usually they don't expose themselves. They do not appreciate human company. It is highly likely that a few moose right now stand somewhere not far away from us and feel our odour with some dismay. I have walked here thousands of times, but one doesn't usually see them, despite the new moose footprints everywhere." I pointed at the soft peat only a metre away. "These footprints are quite fresh. Maybe he walked here just an hour ago."

Just then we heard a powerful flapping of wings, and a huge pitch-black capercaillie cock took off from a treetop just in front of us.

"A capercaillie. In a month there will be a spectacular show going on with the cocks courting the hens."

We passed what I assume is the central point of the peat bog. A circular opening nearly without shrubs. The point at which the ancient lake remained as open water the longest. Here it is very marshy, and it might even be dangerous to walk alone here if one is not knowledgeable about this type of nature. A careless and ignorant person could easily sink down to his waist. From here the vegetation gradually became higher, denser, and more robust in all directions. The blue plastic ribbon markings lead us to slightly more solid ground, and within ten minutes we arrived at the site.

"Well, Anders Andersson. Here it is. As you can see and hopefully agree to, we have put a lot of effort into the digging. Obviously, we wanted to make sure as far as possible that there is not a third victim lying here somewhere."

"An impressive work. All by hand. It is next to impossible to take any machines out here."

They had dug about one metre deep, the area being approximately 20 square metres. A huge undertaking with spades as the only tool. Jan Bengtsson said:

"It was a terrible sight. They lay here next to each other in identical positions. Arms, legs, and necks straight as if they participated in a military parade. Hell! The woman was at least as tall as the man. Both were about 175 centimetres. The man seemed robust while the woman was lean. Her hair was very long, down to her hips. The man also had long hair; he could very well have had a ponytail. The woman was probably a beauty; the teeth were perfect. I suppose they are now trying to determine their ages."

"Yes. I will call Linköping later today, and probably go up there tomorrow. Why on earth were they buried here? How did they get here? Were they executed here, or did someone carry the bodies here? Does the choice of this location suggest that the perpetrators were acquainted with the area? If so, there are not many possible perpetrators to choose between. Did the victims and/or the perpetrators work here? Maybe it cannot be fully excluded, but it seems far-fetched that total strangers would find this place for the execution or for the burial. Anyway, by all probability, the killers are long gone. They escaped justice during their lifetime. Had not this adventurous part-time farmer come up with the impossible idea of growing fodder for moose out here, the bodies would have remained here undisturbed till the end of human civilization."

"Well, much to think about" said Jan B. "Here is a memory stick with a couple of hundred photos."

"Thank you very much Jan. Excellent."

I did not have more to ask about. Jan and Sven followed the markings back to the hunting tower, and then they drove back home to Kalmar after mission completed. I remained on site for at least another half hour. My thoughts wandered here and there without achieving anything constructive. After my moment of contemplation, I took the compass out of the pocket, and walked in the opposite direction, away from The Railway. After coming out of the peat bog 30 minutes later, I used footpaths and little roads I knew so well. I probably know the area better than any other person now after my father passed away. I had a 2-hour-long, wonderful walk back home. I wanted to believe that heaven is a place on earth. Apparently, hell is also a place on earth.

5

Coming home I saw that Saku had sent messages. This was expected, she does that every day. I sent her a few childish chats about a butterfly and a tropical flower. The butterfly crept up and down her so shapely calf and scrutinized it. Saku loved my passion sitting in the backseat being driven home from a board meeting.

I had lunch with Mama in the canteen at the assisted living facility together with the other elderly living there. I knew many of these people, in some cases since my childhood, and we had a pleasant and relaxed time together. After lunch I had coffee with Mama in her nice little one-bedroom apartment. Now was the time to approach old times out in the Wild Moss, and to see if her memory was clear enough to give useful hints for my investigation. I knew she liked to talk about the past.

"Mama, I remember Uncle Nisse. He used to come home to us each evening when I was a child to get the previous day's newspaper. Nisse was his name, wasn't it?"

"Yes! Do you really remember him? Yes, yes! Nisse was his name. Poor Nisse. He did not have a very joyful life."

"Why? Did he have any particular problem? I can't remember."

"He was so lonely when he became old. I believe we were the only people he ever met at that time. And your father didn't really like him."

"I have some vague memory that you or Dad told me that Nisse, long ago, had lived in Kirsta, and that he had worked on extracting peat moss from the Wild Moss. Is that correct?"

"Yes, it is! But it's a long time ago. Nisse and his older brother Edvin built Kirsta when they were young and made peat extraction their livelihood for many years. Later they built the house next to ours, and there Nisse lived the latter part of his life. Edvin lived there too but not for long. The two brothers built other houses nearby also. For example, they built the Vilhelm House. I don't know why that house is called 'the Vilhelm House'. You know which house I talk about?"

"Yes, I do. Just next to the sawmill. Neither do I know who Vilhelm might have been."

"You remember Nisse's brother Edvin? A short, lean, strong, hot-tempered man. An entrepreneur but not easy to get along with. In many ways, Edvin and Nisse had as opposite characters as two men can have. Strange they were brothers. Nisse was slow, corpulent, and he always walked hunching behind Edvin. Nisse was a friendly man, but not smart or alert to be honest."

"I do remember Edvin. When you talk about him, there is a recollection emerging in me. No doubt about it. When approximately did he die?"

"I do not know. After they left Kirsta, we didn't see very much of Edvin. I don't remember anyone ever telling us he had died. But he must have died, we all do. He became sort of a religious extremist. I remember I was told he preached once in a Pentecostal church nearby, but people said he talked so much about punishment and doomsday, that no one wanted to invite him again. The congregation had complained. It seems now, when I think about it, as if Edvin vanished somehow. But I simply don't know. Don't take my words too seriously. I tend to forget these days."

"When you were a child, you lived close to Kirsta and the Wild Moss. About 30 minutes walking distance. For you running it would have been at most five minutes. Did you often meet those living out there?"

"Well, well. It would have taken more than five minutes running. But yes, we were close neighbours. No, we did not meet much. As a matter of fact, I can't remember ever being in Kirsta while it was inhabited. Now, whether your grandparents visited people in Kirsta, that I don't know. Not often anyway. Somehow those people were not members of the community. They were like outsiders."

"Isn't that strange. Why was that? Were you not a tight community with people being together a lot?"

"I don't know what to say. The folks in Kirsta were not very well seen by all. They were left outside. At that time, most people in the area were so very religious in an old-fashioned way. They came to believe that those in Kirsta did not live quite according to the common norm, and that they did not trust in God as one should. Later, as I said, Edvin became a religious extremist, but I think that came only after they left Kirsta. As I remember Edvin from my early childhood, he was not at all religious. He was grumpy, impatient, always in a hurry and usually he seemed a bit angry. We children were not very fond of him though he never did us any harm."

"Do you remember when the peat extraction out in the Wild Moss ended? When they left Kirsta and moved up to Hällerum?"

"You ask and ask. This is difficult. But perhaps, I think they lived up here in Hällerum in the Vilhelm House during the war."

"Hm. Just a few more questions in this interrogation. Were Nisse and Edvin alone in Kirsta? Did they have helpers? Was there no woman?"

"They had seasonal workers. Poor boys. Sometimes some of them came to us during harvest and threshing to make an extra penny if possible. Woman, you said! How could I forget? Helvig! You remember Helvig, don't you? She lived to become old."

Indeed, I remembered Helvig, but I had not known that she, earlier in life, had lived in Kirsta. During my childhood and up into my teens she came walking with her old bicycle loaded with all sorts of rubbish. She walked muttering to herself. She was considered by most to be cranky or even insane, and many laughed behind her back. At the time of my childhood, she was an old woman, she had long straggly hair, and not a single tooth left. She looked like a witch from a cartoon. When she passed by, she came into our kitchen, and Mama always offered her coffee and something to eat.

She didn't talk much. Mama was always kind to Helvig, but we children were afraid of her. We could also be mean. Once, as a friend and I were told Helvig was coming on the road a kilometre away, we placed an empty purse on the road, and attached a string to the purse. We hid in the roadside bushes. When Helvig came walking with her squeaking bicycle, she saw the purse and bowed down to grab it. Then we pulled the string. Helvig screamed in fury and behaved as if totally mad. The same moment we had pulled the string, we regretted what we had done. Mama became furious when she heard what had happened. I had never seen Mama like that. I will not forget how she berated me. Still today I often think of the incident. Bad conscience has plagued me my whole life. To hit the weakest. How cruel kids can be.

"Of course, I remember Helvig. I did a nasty thing to her once. Never have I seen you so angry as then. I'm still ashamed. But in what way was she connected to those in Kirsta?"

"She was maid for Nisse and Edvin, and probably more than that for Edvin. When Helvig was younger, in the mid-1930s, she was a most good-looking woman and definitely not dumb. Long, curly, pitch-black hair. She was probably the one in Kirsta we met the most. She talked as if she had her origin in the northern part of the country, but otherwise I have no idea where she came from. It seemed as if she did not live permanently in Kirsta. She came there for periods. Her skin was beautifully brown, she was tall, and she had a perfect figure. Judging from the way she looked, she probably was a Roma. But I don't know for sure."

"For a few years during the 1930s she came to us regularly for certain seasonal work. Your grandparents liked her a lot, and so did I. She was fun and a nice person. Poverty, and perhaps other setbacks, took a heavy toll on her. She lost all her teeth and at an older age and she hunched more than anyone I've seen. As an old woman she looked like a gnome or a witch, please forgive me for saying so. And full of bitterness somehow. Not towards us because we were always kind to her. I don't know why her fate was so unfortunate. Now I sometimes feel we should have tried to help her more. We should have been more active when we saw what was about to happen to her. Her life became miserable."

"How sad. What a memory you have, Mama. The family name of Nisse and Edvin was Karlsson. Do you remember what Helvig's family name was?"

"Strangely enough I do; her name was Lindberg."

"Do you know where she lived when she was not in Kirsta?"

"That's a good question. But no, I don't think I have ever known that. We did not ask so much those day. Didn't want to intrude. Who could you ask now? Difficult, because now I'm probably the living person who knew Helvig the best. At least in this community."

"Where was she buried? And Nils and Edvin?"

"Nisse was buried in Tuna. Your dad, your grandparents, and I were the only ones at Nisse's funeral. Sad. He had absolutely no friends and apparently no relatives with whom he had contact. I remember how angry I was that no other villagers bothered to pay him some last respect. So, let's see about Edvin and Helvig. No, I do not think I have ever known where they were buried."

"Thanks for the coffee and for the chat, Mama. I will now withdraw. I'll be back when I feel I need another good lunch. By the way, Saku comes here in two-three weeks. At least that is what I hope. Then you will have yet another one to talk to."

"Good. She's so nice. You have been lucky. Thanks for coming."

6

As I came back home the time was 2.30 p.m. which was perfect timing for my afternoon nap. An afternoon nap is a habit I have adopted after my partial retirement. Just dozing for about 30 minutes, and one wakes up as a fully re-energized person. After brushing my teeth and some cold water in the face after the nap, I called Jan N to update him about the developments.

"Anders, it sounds like things are moving on. What an alert mother you have."

"Yes, Mama has always been observant. Open minded and welcoming towards newcomers. A flexible mind somehow. She and my maternal grandfather are my special favourites and role models. I move on with my little investigation. There is usually tailwind the first couple of days in most cases since one starts from close to zero. Let's see how it goes the next two-three weeks. We stay in touch, Jan."

My plan had been to go up to Forensic Medicine in Linköping the next day to see the bodies found in the peat bog and to talk to the people up there. It's a drive of about 70 minutes from my home in Hällerum up to Linköping. However, I changed my mind, and decided instead to simply walk in the Wild Moss and refresh my memory of details of the geography. I wanted to localize the old ditches from which the peat had painstakingly been dug. For example, I wanted to see how far away these ditches are from the site where the bodies were found. I knew it couldn't be far through the dense bushes, but I needed to update myself of details.

I called Forensic Medicine and talked to professor Åsa Svensson.

"Well, Anders, this is not a pleasant sight. The positive part is that we have plenty of material for DNA analysis. I think probably we can discuss more on Wednesday."

"Fine. I need some rest. Any other news?"

"Maybe. We believe the man was around 45, the woman somewhat younger. She was a tall and lean woman, at least 176 centimetres. The hair was dark, if not black, and very long, but you knew that already. Both seem to have been in good health. The woman could have been a Colgate model. The man's teeth were also healthy, though not as perfect. I now estimate their time of burial to sometime between 1930 and 1940."

"Thanks. I'll come up to visit on Wednesday, if OK. We keep in touch."

I sent off a mail to the Support Function of the Central Criminal Investigation Unit asking them to dig out as much as possible from any archive about Nils (Nisse) and Edvin Karlsson, Tuna County, about Helvig Lindberg, and about the property Kirsta in Tuna County.

I started to think about the name Helvig. Such a noble name. An old German name carried by queens, countesses, and other aristocratic women. Was Helvig really the true name of the old, poor, broken-down woman I had known? Why not? When her parents named her, they probably had high hopes for their daughter, and in her youth, according to Mama, Helvig was beautiful and clever with a joyful mindset. Had she lived under more favourable circumstances, she might have educated herself to become a professor of astrophysics and won the Nobel Prize. Two minutes of Googling tells you there are 25 individuals in Sweden today with the name Helvig, but none with the name Helvig Lindberg. Some searching in the archives by professionals should yield results possible to handle.

After having sent off the email, I lit a fire in the tiled stove, and sat down in my most comfortable armchair. I put on the earphones, logged on to Spotify, and listened first to Mozart's *Prague* symphony, and then to Beethoven's *Eroica*. Both recordings from the early 1960s with Karajan conducting the Berlin Philharmonia. After this, to calm down, I selected the slow movements from Beethoven's sonatas *Hammerklavier* and *Pathetique* with Kempff and Brendel, respectively. Then I sat relaxed and did nothing but rest my eyes on the snow-white ceiling for at least an hour.

I plugged the pen drive Jan Bengtsson had given to me into my computer. Many excellent photos. I have seen many gruesome deeds, but one never gets immune to seeing the result of brutality committed by humans on fellow humans. As expected, nothing new of factual significance was revealed by studying the pictures. However, I was overwhelmed by an eerie, utterly scary feeling when seeing the precision and the perfection of the deeds. Indeed, as Jan Bengtsson had said, one got the impression the victims were participating in a military parade. Someone had really bothered to place the bodies in perfect positions.

And the impacts! Horrible! Identical on both victims. One, as it seems, from above into the centre of the skull. The other from behind to a neck vertebra. Same angle, same power on both victims. The murder weapon must have been a perfectly sharp axe handled by a master. Pathological madness.

Just before midnight Sri Lanka time I received a message from Saku: 'I wish my butterfly were here. Now I will sleep with sweet dreams. Talk tomorrow. Hugs from Tropical Flower."

I cooked a superb Tagliatelle Bolognese, grated some first-class Oro del Maso, and had two glasses of a full-bodied red Duoro. I watched news on TV and was in bed already at 21.45.

7

As always, I woke up at 4.30 a.m. This morning I enjoyed a double espresso still sitting in bed with four pillows behind my back. Alternatively, equally often, the first drink I serve myself early morning is black high-grown Ceylon-tea or green or black Pu Erh-tea. As expected, I had a message from Saku: 'My beloved! I'm in the car on my way back to Colombo. Ravi drives calmly and gently, soon I will fall asleep. My butterfly! I hope you have slept well and hidden your wings so that no one has trampled them. They are for me only. Kisses!" Unbelievable! What have I done to deserve this warm and passionate, yet, when needed, calm and analytical woman? The wings of the butterfly are my hands, to which she has taken a particular liking. And indeed, others too have said I have beautiful fingers. They are long and slender, spared hard physical labour. The skin is soft. Saku has asked me why I did not become a medical doctor. She says my touch could have cured disease. Others have said I should have become a pianist.

Just before 900 a.m. I started to walk towards the Wild Moss. The air was crisp, cool but also saturated with moisture. The sky was blue with scattered clouds, and it felt unlikely this day would bring rain. The leaves of the bushes and of the shrubs were soaking wet from morning dew and would probably remain wet till early afternoon. Walking through the landscape out there in the dense vegetation, one would immediately become wet throughout, thus I put on rubber boots and a rainsuit. To reach the burial site, I walked along the blue-ribbon markings from hunting tower eleven, since I was myself not certain how to get to the dig unaided, for example, from the Kirsta remains, although that should be closer. It is easy indeed to get lost in this area. Arriving at the site I sat down on the stool built-in to my rucksack and had coffee and sweet chocolate biscuits. I sat one metre away from the edge of the impressive dig.

What happened here? Were the victims executed just here or in the immediate vicinity, or were the bodies dragged or carried here? Did one watch the first being killed waiting for his/her turn? If they had been dragged here after having been killed, in sacks of some sort, the sacks would have become soiled with blood, and the reasonable thing would have been that the sacks had been buried, gotten rid of, together with the bodies.

Jan Bengtsson and his helpers had put enormous efforts into the digging but found nothing except for the bodies and the clothes on the bodies. Had the dead bodies been dragged here by the killers or by horses without being wrapped in sacks or whatever, then we should find damage to the clothes, or injuries to the bodies. Definitely on the woman's long hair. I must ask Forensic Medicine if they have seen any signs of this. These days it is next to impossible to come out here with a tractor or even a horse, and those days, 70—80 years ago, the ground was probably even more marshy than today. During a cold winter, with the ground frozen, it would be different. Then it would likely have been possible to come here with a horse and a sledge. On the other hand, during winter with snow and the ground frozen, digging graves to hide away the bodies would have been a formidable task without advanced tools.

I can't see a way for us to find out during which season the murders were committed and the graves dug. The bodies had not simply been thrown into their graves but placed with precision next to each other after having been executed identically. Some sort of ritual? Religious madness? Well, I can sit philosophizing like this until I go crazy myself. I need facts if there are any.

I took my compass and my 25-year-old map out of the rucksack. On this map, many years ago, I had marked the sites where impact on nature from the extraction of peat can still be seen. These remains consisted of 15 man-made ditches. The ditches were of impressive dimensions; up to 75 metres long, perfectly straight, 3–4 metres broad, and 1–2 metres deep. The sides of some of the ditches still today are nearly vertical. The ditches run parallel in a north-south direction, with only 2–3 metres between them. The beds of the ditches today are covered by about ½ metre deep brown water. Would someone happen to fall into one of these ditches, that unfortunate person would be in serious trouble. He/she would helplessly sink into the mire, and if alone on a walk, probably be beyond rescue. I have not heard of any deadly accident out here with humans involved during my lifetime, but both moose and cattle are known to have drowned in the ditches.

Now I sat on the stool at the burial site, and I tried to set the compass in the direction towards the ditches. I was not fully sure of the exact position of the burial site, thus the direction towards the ditches was partly guesswork. However, should I miss the ditches, I could turn straight south, and then soon reach The Railway. I kept the compass in front of me and started walking. The thicket, mainly birch and pine and in some areas, fir trees, was mostly about 2½ metres high, each leaf or needle still saturated with morning dew to at least double its weight, and it became more and more dense as I walked. I held my arms in front of me like a snowplough and checked the compass every second metre. On some stretches, I could see no more than 30 centimetres in front of me. Without a rainsuit this would have been most uncomfortable. The ground was marshy and difficult. For each step I had to watch where to put my foot to avoid sinking. I proceeded very slowly. After fifteen minutes, the thicket became less dense, and the ground firmer. I could speed up somewhat. Suddenly, I saw one of the ditches not more than three metres in front of me. I had reached the easternmost extent of the 15 ditches.

I was astonished. I had thought the ditches would be at least three times further away from the burial site. Now, in fact, the burial site and the ditches are only 250, maximally 300, metres apart. Here, a group of people had worked at the time the graves were dug. Seventy to eighty years ago much in the surroundings must have been different. The shrubs most probably shorter and less dense, if at all in existence. Such is the evolution of a peat bog. Screams and loud noises would be heard from one site to the other. Maybe I should consult an expert on peat bog geology and natural development to get a scientifically based understanding of what it may have looked like around 1935. Perhaps there was nearly a clear view from the workplace at the ditches to the graves. The ground is flat as a pancake. My goodness!

I walked onto the three metres broad strip of reasonably firm ground between the second and the third ditch. Again, I sat down on my rucksack, and took out the thermos with coffee. I had been in the immediate vicinity of this place many times. When I was about 15, not more than 200 metres to the north, I built a nice hideaway in which to sit early mornings during March and April to observe and to film capercaillie cocks courting their ladies.

Were possibly the horrible things that happened here sometime between 1930 and 1940 the reason why the inhabitants fled Kirsta and the commercial extraction of peat came to an end? Was that why Nisse and Edvin built new houses in Hällerum? Did these events make Edvin become somewhat of a religious fanatic and soon disappear from the neighbourhood, and Helvig to become embittered and seemingly lose her mind?

Why had not Edvin, Nisse, or Helvig alarmed the police about the heinous crimes? Were they afraid the same would happen to them, or did they feel obliged to protect someone? Were they themselves, or at least one or two of them, involved in the crime? Or was it only a coincidence the bodies were buried this close to their place of work? Maybe the folks in Kirsta and those working out on the peat bog had no knowledge about the matter.

8

The next few days I relaxed. I listened to music, at least three times to the exceptional 'Portraits in Jazz' with Bill Evans Trio from 1960. How amazingly elegant and refined! Not least, the bassist Scott LaFaro is phenomenal. Paving the way for later bassists I admire so much. Sunday evening, I rounded up with a Jimi Hendrix-orgy. 'The Third Stone from the Sun', 'Are You Experienced', and selected parts of 'Electric Ladyland' pleasantly influence my mind each time I listen. I had lunch with Mama on Friday, and I took her to a restaurant in Vimmerby on Saturday. During Sunday I visited both my sisters.

There wasn't too much I could do except wait for results from ongoing investigations. My brain worked rather irrationally. I thought of the murders out on the peat bog, but I did not achieve much. My goal was first and foremost to find out who the victims were. It is difficult even to imagine it will be possible to prove who were the perpetrators. But we will see. It happens in investigations that unexpected breakthroughs or setbacks come when you least expect them. Sometimes, a case which appears hopeless takes a giant leap forward, while in other cases, where you have nearly all answers and facts to start with, the final piece of evidence proves elusive.

I had a chat with Saku every day. Mainly about butterflies climbing the tropical flower. Saku was an exceptional and passionate, on occasion an egocentric, lover. She allowed me to admire her. She gave to her partner through accepting compliments and thereby becoming ecstatic. How I loved this generous surrender mixed with egoism!

Monday afternoon, as I sat staring at my computer, an email arrived from professor Åsa Svensson at Forensic Medicine in Linköping.

"Hi Anders! We are not quite done yet with the evaluation of the DNA tests, but I couldn't wait to inform you about the following: The murdered woman was a Roma. She and the murdered man were not related. His DNA is typical ethnic Scandinavian. But that is not all; the woman had DNA from this man in her vagina. Probably they had intercourse not long before they were killed. On top of that she was approximately six weeks into pregnancy. The murdered man was the father. The woman had probably given birth at least once. That's that. Interesting I would assume. Regarding your question about other smaller injuries on the bodies, or signs of impact on the clothes, I can say we see no such impact. The woman's waist-long hair was as if newly combed, and we don't find bruises on the skin anywhere on either one of them."

I sat baffled and disgusted in front of my computer for minutes after I had read the email from Åsa. It's getting worse and worse. What could have led to this madness? A frenzied jealousy drama? A religious ritual to clean the earth of Satan? This region has always been plagued by extreme, flaky preachers visiting the many small houses of worship scattered all over, preaching hell and punishment. I myself had to listen to much idiocy during my childhood. Men in black suits warning and threatening uneducated people how easy it was to end up in hell for all eternity. Most people visiting these houses of worship were genuinely good, very ordinary people wishing everybody all the best. However, many of these had no intellectual self-confidence, but instead an over-reliance on 'authorities' and 'superiors'. God, the King, and the rich, in that order. Many were easily led into mad variants of religious beliefs.

Well, the murdered woman was a Roma. Åsa's statements are always true. Mama thought that Helvig possibly was a Roma, and she is also usually very trustworthy. Helvig and the woman in the grave thus could very well have been related. The burial sites of Edvin and Helvig are so far unknown. What I can do now, while waiting for results from the studies into the archives, is to ask for permission to open Nisse Karlsson's grave, and make DNA analysis to see if he was related to any of the victims. It was such a small group of people spending their days out on the Wild

48

Moss, so it is not far-fetched to assume they had some connection to the deeds or to the victims, even if they are not necessarily guilty of any crime.

I enjoyed chicken breast fillet in tomato sauce, a recipe I have refined all my life. Each fillet cut into two, and with slits to facilitate the absorption of the flavours. Onions, as much garlic I happen to have in the house, oregano, basil, lots of black pepper, a beef cube, some red wine, a can of crushed tomatoes and some water. The liquid reduces so that it thickens somewhat and so that the chicken meat gets very well cooked, close to being fragmented and saturated with taste. Boiled or roasted potatoes and two glasses of a full-bodied Alentejo or Duoro. Saku loves the dish, and she is most seductive when she enjoys it. Now, in my loneliness, when the second glass was half empty, I called Jan Norberg's private phone.

"Hi Anders! A call from you so soon again. I understand the investigation has moved on."

"Yes, but I don't have a clear grip in which direction it goes. I want to talk for a few minutes. The whole thing has become even nastier."

I informed Jan of the developments. Jan has a rare ability to state truisms in a way that makes him sound brilliant. I have never heard him come up with anything new, or something that my other colleagues and I had not thought of more or less from the start of an investigation. Still, one felt stimulated after having talked to him. He is most sympathetic. He usually chairs press conferences due to his position in the hierarchy, but he never claims credit for important achievements in the investigations. He always takes utmost care so that the right officer gets the acclaim.

"Well, well Anders, that's something! I definitely think you should try and sort out a possible relationship between Nisse Karlsson and the victims. Both negative and positive outcomes would give important information. I support you fully if now my support is of any importance."

"Your support is important. Thank you so much Jan. I will come up to Stockholm rather soon. I will drop by at your office, and hopefully we can have lunch or a dinner together. Best regards to Greta! Or why don't the two of you come here? I will cook something nice for you."

"Thanks Anders. I will probably remain seated here for at least another month. Nice if we could meet up here."

10

Already Thursday the same week, I stood at the edge of Nisse Karlsson's grave and saw how the remains were uncovered. The permissions were easy to obtain since there were no known relatives to ask. The caretaker of the cemetery had quickly localized the grave. 'Nils Karlsson, Karlsborg, Hällerum, 1890–1967'. Karlsborg was the name, largely forgotten, of the house that was the nearest neighbour to my home. So, I was 17 when he died. Then I was in high school in Hultsfred, and at home only during weekends. I was away many weekends too, since at that time I played chess at a rather advanced level. The skeleton looked somehow neat and well organised, not like the rather corpulent and clumsy man I remember. At last, the friendly man had come to rest. One assistant, Pia Nilsson, had come down from Forensic Medicine in Linköping to collect material for the investigations.

"Nice work, Pia. When do you think we can expect the results?"

"In about a week. We don't have much of a queue, thus it could be faster. I'll prioritize this for tomorrow."

"Excellent. I suggest we now have lunch in Vimmerby. There is an Indian/Chinese/Thai/Indonesian restaurant at the main square. They even usually have some traditional Swedish dishes. Food is really nice."

After a good lunch, I returned home and sat in my kitchen with coffee and chocolate biscuits. Having nothing better to do, I opened my computer, mainly to have a chat with Saku should she happen to be available, but I saw there was an email from the Support Function at the Central Criminal Police. It was a long email, full of details. They had dug deeply into all existing archives. The most important pieces of information were:

1. Helvig Lindberg: One single person carrying that name had been found. That person was born 1892 in Sorsele, Lapland. Date and place of death had not been recorded. The family were Romas, but it seemed they had settled permanently in Sorsele about the time when Helvig was born. Helvig had a sister six years younger, Alvina Lindberg. Helvig was employed in a grocery store in Sorsele 1905–1910. Helvig's and Alvina's mother died 1909, and from 1910 no trace of the sisters could be found in any archive. Helvig and Alvina had many relatives on the father's side, and the email contained addresses and telephone numbers to two children of first cousins, and the same information for twelve grandchildren of first cousins. These relatives

were spread all over the country, but one branch of the family still lived in Sorsele.

2. Edvin and Nils Karlsson: Edvin, born 1888, and Nils, born 1890, would, according to the archives, have a younger brother named Vilhelm, born 1893. There was nothing in the archives suggesting the brothers would have had any first cousins, or that they ever married or had children. Vilhelm emigrated to America 1910 and settled in northern Minnesota in a county called Freetown. The county is bordering Canada. Even the name of the administrative capital of the county, the name of the present mayor, Peter Karl, and the telephone number to the office of the mayor, were included in the email.

3. Further results of the investigations showed that Edvin Karlsson sold the property Kirsta in February 1938. A month earlier he had bought a plot of land in nearby Hällerum. He sold this plot 1941, and then bought another piece of land in Hällerum. From details given I could identify the first plot of land Edvin bought in Hällerum as the land where the so-called Vilhelm House was built. The second plot of land he bought is where the house called Karlsborg now stands. Karlsborg is where Nisse Karlsson lived the latter part of his life all alone and it is also the nearest neighbour to my childhood home.

Mama does not know of the brother Vilhelm. Obviously, Nisse never talked about him, despite sitting on a chair in our kitchen for a while almost every evening during many years. Nisse was a man of few words, but still it is a bit odd that he never mentioned his brother who had emigrated. Was that sensitive for some reason? Anyway, now I knew why the house on the other side of the sawmill was called the Vilhelm House.

I called Britt-Marie on the Support Function to express my appreciation. I had worked with Britt-Marie on many investigations since the early days of my career, and I knew she always works tirelessly.

"Britt-Marie! You have achieved a lot in a short time. Please extend my thanks to the whole team. How are you and your family?"

"We are just fine thank you so much. Well, we are here not only to do crosswords. Everyone here knows that you appreciate engagement and that you are no stranger to giving credit to those who work hard. It was exciting to work that far back in time, and all the way over to the North American wilderness. It is wilderness up there, isn't it?"

"Yes. Full of grizzly and other wild game also I suppose. Several First Nations in the area. I have been in Minnesota but never all the way up at the Canadian border. I was in Duluth once to visit a cousin of my grandmother. I came from Chicago on a Harley Davidson, and I had a nice gal sitting behind. An adventure of my youth. I had no time to go further up north."

"Let me know if there is anything more we can do. Probably we can find out more about Vilhelm in America, but methods I'm not so used to may be needed. Now I must finish off one thing, and later tonight I will play bridge."

"Thanks again Britt-Marie. Thanks to you I have something to do. Otherwise, I might have started climbing the walls. Almost certainly I will come back with more requests."

In the evening I drove to Mama with the leftovers of my masterpiece on chicken, and the half bottle remaining of the Alentejo. We heated the food in the micro while watching news on TV. She commended my cooking, but she was also thoughtful. She had read in the newspaper about the events.

"What a horrible thing someone did out there in the Wild Moss. I was probably not far away as it happened."

"No. We believe it happened between 1930 and 1940. You came to Hällerum 1932, didn't you?"

"Yes, we came 1932, I was not yet six. There is one thing I should have told you before: Some of those living in Kirsta sometimes came up to us in those days at harvest-time to earn a few kronor. We had no camera, and I can't believe they had a camera in Kirsta either. However, on several occasions a photographer from Vimmerby came out to us. He wanted to document country-life. We were very respectful towards him because he seemed to have quite advanced equipment.

He was a nice and friendly man. I don't remember his name, but strangely I do remember he came from Johansson's Photo Ltd on Sevedegatan. I think you know where that is. If nothing has changed most recently, there is still a photo studio there. Maybe they have saved old photos from Hällerum and from many other places. He may even have been in Kirsta. I don't know, but he travelled around a lot."

"Mama! You are brilliant! You should have become a Criminal Investigator! I will check it up immediately. I have another question. Did you know that Helvig had a younger sister called Alvina? Do you have any recollection that you ever met someone who could have been Helvig's sister?"

Mama took time to search through her memory. How typical of her! She was silent for at least half a minute.

"I'm ashamed of my poor memory. But yes! Helvig did bring a friend; she may have been her sister. I believe I saw her just once. They were very much alike. The friend was a bit younger. I don't remember if her name was Alvina."

11

At eleven in the evening, I started listening to Bach's piano music. Gould, Richter, Argerich, Nikolajeva. I couldn't stop. Virtuosity from the interpreters and magical genius from the composer. What did it sound like when Bach himself played these masterpieces on the instruments available at that time? Was he a virtuoso like the best pianists of our time? Could he even imagine how fantastic it would sound 300 years later? Could he ever dream of how he would influence the future? I couldn't sleep, and at 2.00 a.m. I sent a message to my tropical flower. It was 6.30 in Colombo, and at that time she is almost always awake. "My flower! I think of you. Call me if you can." Fifteen seconds later she called on Skype.

"Butterfly, you should be deep in sleep at this time."

"I have listened to Bach, and when I closed my eyes, I saw you standing in front of me. You are so beautiful!"

"It's lovely. I like so much to be beautiful for you. I have changed profoundly since I met you. I take great care with lipstick and all other things even when you are not here. I want all to know that you have found such a beautiful woman, and that she has made you a much happier person!"

"Saku! What can I say? I love you!"

"I love you! Now I must get on with my morning. Today Ravi will take me to Batticaloa, and I will stay for a few days. I hope to come to you in about two weeks. I will take great care what I have on so that you will like what you see."

At nine Friday morning I stood at the entrance of Johansson's Photo on Sevedegatan in Vimmerby. Later this day I would start calling Helvig's relatives, and in the evening even try to reach the mayor in Minnesota. Finally, I have some meaningful things to do.

An elderly man unlocked the door from inside a few minutes after nine.

"I apologise for being late. Not often do we have customers this early. Of course, one should open on time anyway. Welcome!"

After a few greetings I showed my police ID and went straight to the point.

"I have been told that a photographer who documented country life around Vimmerby used to work here. It is some time ago, 1920–1950. Is this correct?"

"Oh yes! Kjell Johansson. He founded this photo studio in 1922. He was born in November 1899 and died in February 2000. Not many have seen three centuries and two millennia. We were together a lot for many years. A passionate photographer. Very few around here even had a camera in 1922. I bought the business from him in 1970 and sold it 12 years ago. Still, I help out here sometimes. Now a single mother with two kids runs the show."

"How interesting! Kjell Johansson must have seen much. The country changed so profoundly from the 1920s and 40–50 years on."

"Yes indeed. He had an eye for everything piquant and special. A professional and artistic photographer."

"I work on trying to clarify the circumstances around a double murder committed in the vicinity of Hällerum sometime during the 1930s. Do photos from that time and place remain? I might get valuable clues from seeing them."

"I have good news for you. Kjell's whole archive is stored and taken well care of by one of his granddaughters, Anita Berggren. She is a housewife, and she lives close to Örebro in a big villa. A very well organised and nice person. Now after the children have moved out, she has devoted much time to organising and archiving the stuff. I have seen the archive which occupies two rooms in the basement. If there are relevant photos, you will have a good chance of finding them."

"Finally, things happen! Can you give me her phone number?"

"Of course. Welcome to the office for a cup of coffee. By the way, Anita's husband, Jan-Christer, is almost a colleague of yours. A high-up in the Kumla Prison organisation. A bit snobbish if I may say so. Forget I said that. Anita is genuinely nice and pleasant."

12

Anita Berggren answered on the first signal. I explained the situation.

"You are most welcome. I'm almost always at home. Finally, someone is interested in this treasure, be it for unpleasant reasons. Grandpa's life's work. I know there are many photos from Hällerum because I have been through it all."

Anita was born and raised in Vimmerby but had lived in the Örebro area most of her adult life. Her dialect now was an almost comical mixture of the two quite broad and profiled dialects. She talked energetically with a loud voice, and she was most welcoming and positive. We agreed I would show up at their home at 9.00 a.m. next day, a Saturday.

"We will be home. Janne will be busy with the house and with the apple trees, and I will do just normal things. Next week I will look after the grandchildren, so probably I will bake buns. Let's have a simple lunch tomorrow. You can work on your own without me disturbing, but I will have time to help if needed. I have equipment to make paper copies from negatives."

I revised my plans for the day and for the weekend, and I called Åsa at Forensic Medicine in Linköping. We decided to have lunch together, and thereafter I would view the human remains found in the Wild Moss for the first time, then work in an office at Forensic Medicine for a few hours. During the early evening I would drive from Linköping to Örebro Town Hotel, a drive of about two hours.

Seeing the bodies revealed nothing new. Jan Bengtsson's many excellent photos had told it all. However, I had a strong feeling of the pathological and perverted forces that must have been the drivers. A sacrificial rite? I thought for a moment I would throw up. The sculls split identically. The same vertebrae in both victims impacted in exactly the same way. Åsa seemed to read my thoughts and feelings:

"Yes, it is extraordinary. How on earth was this done? The victims must have been locked in a position so that they were unable to move a millimetre. That's the only way for some lunatic to achieve this precision. It is impossible to imagine that the man holding the axe, or whatever tool it was, acted alone."

Just as Jan Bengtsson had said, the woman was tall and lean. The hair reached the hips. Is this Alvina Lindberg? The woman lying here had given birth at least once, so where were the children at the time of the executions? If Alvina had given birth at a young age, the child/children would have been young adults, and they might have been anywhere. Was it these deeds of evil that had made Helvig lose her senses? Maybe she saw the thing happen, unable to do anything about it, and afterwards for some reason was prevented from reporting to the police. Perhaps she had reported to the police but been dismissed as being insane or at least not trustworthy, which may have sped up her deterioration mentally and physically.

I walked into the lab and talked to Pia Nilsson who was occupied with extracting DNA from the bones collected from Nisse Karlsson.

"It goes well. I will obtain excellent DNA patterns from these bones. We have perfect patterns from the victims also. No contaminations at all."

13

At 2.30 p.m. I sat down in the office Åsa had offered me at the Institute of Forensic Medicine and connected my computer. I would now start calling some of Helvig's relatives on the list provided by Britt-Marie and her colleagues at the Support Function. I started with one of Helvig's and Alvina's first cousin's children. The name of this man was Hugo Lindberg, and he lived in Sorsele in Lapland, but not at the same address as the one where Helvig and Alvina had lived. The voice answering my call sounded as if it belonged to a teenage girl.

"Oh yes, I will go and get great grandpa. He's out here somewhere. It may take a minute."

After a while I heard sounds as if someone walked with heavy shoes on an old-fashioned wooden floor.

"Hello. Hugo Lindberg speaking. Who am I talking to?"

I explained my errand. Hugo, who according to my information would be 89 years of age, seemed to have healthy hearing and a good ability to comprehend. Not once did I have to repeat myself, and twice he asked quite reasonable questions for clarification.

"That was quite a story! I'm not sure I can help you much. But yes, my grandfather had an elderly brother who had two daughters."

"But you never met them?"

"No. My Grandfather's brother died long before I was born, and I suppose the girls moved south as almost all others. I never saw them, at least not as far as I can remember."

"But you heard people talk about them?"

"My father talked a few times about his dead uncle whom he did not like at all. He said his uncle, that is the father of the girls, was a nasty and a bad man. He was almost always drunk, and his wife was forced to walk the streets begging. Dad said the eldest of the girls worked at an early age to help the mother, but the evil bastard consumed that money too. He hit the girls if they objected. My father also said the girls' mother was a very good woman, and that she was good looking when she was young. He said she was the most beautiful girl in the entire south Lapland. She died early; I think it says 1909 on the tombstone. If I remember correctly, my father said that his uncle's evil nature probably was what made his wife die early, and that he should have been put in prison. Maybe the girls fled from their father when the mother died. It seemed that my father felt ashamed the family didn't do more to help the mother and the girls, but he did not want to talk much about it."

"That sounds bad indeed. Did your father say if the cousins were tall or short?"

"Yes. He said they were tall and lean just like their mother."

"Is your family Roma?"

"We are. My Grandpa and his brother settled here permanently. Later generations have mixed blood but the girls you query about were full-blooded Roma. I am too."

"Do you know if anyone else in the extended family could help me further? Usually there is someone in most families who is passionate about taking care of old photos and other old things."

"Yes, we too had such a family member. My sister Isabel. Isabel is unfortunately not with us any more, but her daughter Maja has taken over. Her name is now Maja Kinnunen. She lives in Sundsvall. She is married to some big shot in the paper industry, and she herself is a bank director, regional head of some major bank I believe. They are very well off. Most of the old family photos are with her. My Grandpa was one of the first in Lapland to own a camera, and my Dad inherited the interest in shooting photos. I myself have never owned a camera. Maja probably has photos of the entire extended family."

"You do not happen to remember the names of your father's beautiful cousins?"

"No. There may be some document here somewhere. If I search the whole house, I may find something. If so, I promise to get back to you. I can give you Maja's phone number and address now in half a minute. I know where those are."

The old man talked to someone in the room and asked for the contact details of Maja Kinnunen. Maja was on my list of Helvig's cousins' grandchildren I had obtained from the Support Function, and the mobile number and address Hugo now gave me were in perfect agreement with what I already had.

"Hugo! Thank you! You have helped me a lot. One last question: Do you know where your grandfather's brother and his wife are buried? I mean the parents of the sisters who went missing."

"Yes, I do. They are buried in the cemetery here in Sorsele. My wife was a firm believer, and she always put fresh flowers on many graves and kept them tidy. I too try to clean up a few times a year."

"Thanks again so much Hugo. We will probably meet in the not-so-distant future. I will try to find out what happened to the girls."

Now there is a way to test if the murdered woman most probably is Alvina Lindberg, or to prove she is not. I have several things to do. Look at photos in Örebro and in Sundsvall, apply for permission to unearth the remains of Helvig's and Alvina's presumed parents and organise all those practical details. I must call Minnesota and possibly follow up on that if it turns out to be promising. I would need more resources at my disposal to make everything happen quickly, but I will not request that. I go for it on my own. This is archaeology in a way. The police have other matters of vital importance for the society to deal with. This is becoming my private passion. I feel such deep sympathy for Helvig and Alvina. I want to know. I am so much ashamed over what I did to Helvig. How I joined the scornful — I regret it so much.

14

I had a nap in the resting room at Forensic Medicine, and shortly before 6.00 p.m. I dialled the number to Maja Kinnunen. Maja answered after a while. Her voice was soft, and she spoke calmly, not forced, and seemingly with self-assurance. She would not easily make herself heard in a noisy environment like sitting with a group of people in a bar with background music. I couldn't prevent myself from thinking the voice was highly sensual. A slight northern accent could be heard, and the vocabulary was highly refined. I introduced myself and continued:

"I have spoken to your uncle Hugo Lindberg, and he said you might have a collection of old family photos in your possession. Is that correct?"

"It is correct. I have saved and tried to organise most of the photos from my Granddad and Great Granddad. I think it is important to save and cherish those things. I even have my Great Granddad's first camera in my collection. I have been told he was the second person in the whole of Lapland to own a camera. You say you are Chief Investigator at the Criminal Police! I hope nothing bad has happened."

"Not recently, but in the past unfortunately. I try to investigate a double murder committed not far from Vimmerby sometime during the 1930s. I will tell more if and when we meet, but one of the victims might have been a relative of yours. This is as yet a hypothesis which might prove to be wrong."

"Of course, I will do what I can to help. May I ask which person it is about?"

"Your maternal Grandfather's father had a brother who had two daughters, Helvig and Alvina Lindberg. It might be that Alvina was one of the victims. I need all available facts about her, including what she looked like. There is more to say but let's talk more when we meet. Did you know of the existence of Helvig and Alvina Lindberg?"

"Oh yes, but they are almost like mythical beings, and a nagging bad conscience for the family. It seems they disappeared around 1910, the year after their mother died, and no one in the family knows a thing of their fate. This was all long before I was born. My maternal Granddad, he was the girls' first cousin, often talked about them. It burdened him heavily that they just disappeared. The girls' father is said to have been an evil man, so maybe they fled him after their mother had died. That's what people believed. The extended family have felt much shame that the girls did not get better support. Many don't want to talk about this."

"Everything is easier in hindsight. Do you have photos of the girls?"

"Many. Many together with their mother. Alvina was just a child. If I remember correctly, she was born 1898. I have no photo of their father."

"It is correct, according to the information I have, that Alvina was born 1898. I would like to see the photos as soon as possible if I may. What about Sunday? Day after tomorrow?"

"I will help as much as I can. You are most welcome. But please, Sunday is not the best day. The weekends when both my husband and I are at home, we want to spend the time together just the two of us. What about Monday afternoon? I can take the afternoon off from work. One o'clock?"

"Fine. I so much look forward to seeing the girls in their childhood. I met Helvig myself many times when I was a child, and she was an old woman. She was somehow embittered and deteriorated both mentally and physically. At that time, she did not have a good life."

"Oh dear. How sad. See you on Monday. I look forward to it."

That sounds great. They will spend the whole of Sunday in bed. I have full understanding. Maybe a walk or a jogging tour in the nature. Maja sounds mild, but at the same time it seems she knows very well what she wants, and that she expects to get what she wants. Thus, tomorrow Saturday I will visit Anita Berggren in Örebro and view old photos from Hällerum and hopefully from Kirsta. Sunday could be spent in Stockholm. Why not have dinner with my daughter and of course meet Jan Norberg for a coffee sometime during the day if he has time for it. Monday morning the northbound train to Sundsvall. I can park the car at Jan's place. A couple of chats with Saku. It all fits perfectly!

15

Anita and Jan-Christer Berggren lived in a big, yellow house, built entirely out of wood, at a lakeshore about 5 kilometres from Örebro. A large slot of land belonged to the house, and they had at least two dozen fruit trees; apple, plum, pear, cherry; all looking healthy and productive. A medium-sized motorboat was moored to a robust bridge. The house was surprisingly isolated considering the proximity to a relatively large town. No neighbouring house was within eyesight. The lake was rather small, but it was connected to the much larger Lake Hjälmaren via a strait. Anita was an alert and nice woman. The black hair must be tinted. She had broad hips, but she moved effortlessly and energetically.

"What about a cup of coffee before we start with the archives? I have buns baked less than an hour ago."

"Thank you so much. The Town Hotel in Örebro offered me a great breakfast buffet, but an oven-warm bun with coffee is always a delicacy."

"You could just as well have stayed here overnight. Why didn't I think of that? We have several empty bedrooms now after the kids have moved out. We must think of that if you return sometime."

The husband Jan-Christer was more of a phlegmatic type. He knew my name and my reputation, and he showed respect. The relationship between the married couple was like between old friends who have accepted each other. A somewhat lukewarm companionship. A type of relationship that I, throughout my life, have had difficulties to get adjusted to. This side of my personality has many times made my life difficult. I can't live without passion. In a way I felt envy towards Anita and Jan-Christer for coming to rest with such a life. Jan-Christer's contribution to our conversation was largely of the type: "Almost all heavy criminals we get to the prison these days have their roots in the Balkans. We have made a mess of our country." After 20 minutes with coffee and buns, Anita and I descended the stairs down to the basement.

"I have prepared for you. All I could find in the archive relating to Hällerum from 1920 and up to the 1950s is here on this table. The red binders contain paper copies, some from my grandfather, some copied from the old negatives by me. The green binders contain the negatives, and the boxes larger negative glass plates and similar things that I not always know how to categorize. Everything is organised chronologically, at least that is the ambition. I am working on a register, and I have recently even taken a computer course so that hopefully I will be able to digitalize the register. I can show you later where I stand with that if we have time."

The sight of the archive stunned me. I couldn't find a suitable way to express my admiration.

"My good Lord what a treasure! I could be on some photos from the 1950s myself. I have been told that my Granddad tied me on to the sowing machine pulled by his magnificent horse. Few inventions on this planet are as noisy as an old-fashioned sowing machine in action, but there I sat sleeping on that thing behind the horse."

The archive was utterly impressive. Two average-sized rooms, from floor to ceiling full of binders and boxes. Everything seemed meticulously labelled. A third smaller room with a computer and printers on two desks served as office. Yet another room had been transformed into a darkroom, seemingly well equipped. On the wall in the office hung a large, framed portrait of Kjell Vide Johansson. On one of the tables, Anita had piled up a number of binders and three boxes.

"I leave you now. Come up at any time for coffee and a bun. If I'm not in, I'm in the garden helping Janne. We will go shopping during the day, but I'll tell you when we leave. I have equipment to view negatives. Ask at any time if you need help. And, as said, my dark room is fairly well equipped, thus I can make paper copies from any negative. I'm so glad someone is here to take advantage of it. Oh, I almost forgot to say that on the backside of the paper copies, or on a separate little sheet of paper in the holder, you find the names of persons on the photo. Not always but many times."

"Anita! This is so fantastic! How could I ever thank you?"

"I'm so happy. Or maybe one shouldn't be happy given the reason for you being here. Maybe you can advise me how to save this for the future."

I opened a binder labelled 'Hällerum 1933'. The binder contained subsections, and I opened one called "Harvesting potatoes on the Stone Field in October." I became emotional. Twenty-five or so years later, I myself dug potatoes out of the soil on the 'Stone Field." Immediately something of immense interest! One of the first photos I focused on showed the whole team of workers. Four women kneeling in the soil, and behind them stood four men and two women. Behind the group one sees high haulm of potato. On the right-hand side of the women in the front row stood a basket containing coffee, other drinks, mugs, and some sort of buns. In front of all lies Mama flat on the soil! No doubt about it. Already then, seven years old, she was recognizable beyond any doubt. Grandma and Granddad are also on the photo. I could not identify the others. My attention was drawn particularly to one of the women standing in the second row. Tall and lean. The woman by her side reached her shoulder. She was seen at an angle; thus, one could see that the hair was tied in a ponytail. The hair was long, black, curly, reaching below the waist. Could this be Helvig? She looked very much like a Roma. This beautiful and charismatic person 25 years later transformed into someone broken down, extremely hunched, witch-like and embittered. At a closer look, maybe after all there is some similarity with the aged Helvig. The hawk-like expressive profile. I must show this photo to Mama and compare it with photos from Maja Kinnunen's collection. Oh yes, I almost forgot! Anita told me the names of persons often were noted somewhere. And indeed! As I removed the photo from the holder, I discovered a folded sheet of paper. The tall woman was Helvig Lindberg! The shortest of the men was Nils Karlsson. I could not have guessed this man was Nils, despite the fact I saw him almost daily 20 years later. Grandma, Granddad and Mama were correctly named. The other names were unknown to me. It was not sensational that Helvig and Nisse were on the photo since Mama had said that folks from Kirsta now and then came to do seasonal work. Still, I was strongly moved by the photo. I could not hold back tears. Helvig! What a hellish life you had led so far with your evil father, and what a hellish life lay in front of you! You would be forced to meet mean little boys. People laughed behind your back. Helvig, forgive me! I'm ashamed and I regret it. Many more should have helped you. How beautiful and strong you were! How I wish life had been kind to you.

I sat in the archive for three hours, and I walked up the stairs once for coffee and buns. Almost as in the good old days when Mama baked. I carefully went through the material Anita had put on the table, and I found many photos with Helvig and Nisse, and one from

1928 on which also Nils' older brother Edvin appeared. Edvin was less than medium tall, on the borderline of being skinny, and he looked very energetic. This was the complete opposite to Nils who was corpulent and always looked half asleep. Despite the differences in overall body shape, similarities in facial features were obvious. Many photos were immensely beautiful, shot as they were by a professional. Here was a fantastic documentation of country life in the 1920s up to the 1950s.

The last binder I looked into before dinner was labelled, 'Harvesting and threshing in Hällerum 1937'. Here I found one photo showing the whole team of workers, 25 persons, lined up in three rows with an impressive smorgasbord visible behind them. I recognised the location. It was in the garden just in front of my Grandparents' house though the house was not seen on the photo. In my childhood, I played in that garden hundreds of times. In 1937 the two apple trees appearing on the photo had their heydays, while in my memory from my childhood and teens they were old and gnarled. I knew these two trees now have been felled, since I had passed the house on the narrow gravel road in my car just a week earlier. No sheet of paper with names of the persons was available for this photo. Helvig and Nisse were present, I had learnt to recognise them the way they looked at that time. As I scrutinised the group further, all of a sudden I felt unstable, and got goose bumps all over. Another one! On the far right in the back row. A younger copy of Helvig! So much alike but visibly younger! The same wonderful hair. As tall and the same body shape. The same discrete and charming smile. The characteristic profile. Who can this be if not Alvina?

Anita had invited me to stay for dinner, and, if I so wanted, to stay overnight. I accepted the invitation, and I managed to book meetings with my daughter and with Jan Norberg in Stockholm during the afternoon and evening next day which was a Sunday.

At dinner I expressed my admiration for the archive, and how satisfied I was with the results of the day, and how thankful I was with the help provided by Anita and Jan-Christer.

"It's an outstanding collection. A museum could be built. What a treasure!"

"Yes, isn't it remarkable? The achievement of a lifetime of passion and skill. We will see what can happen to it all eventually. I really don't know."

"Only one more thing was on my wish list, namely some photos from what we call the Wild Moss. That's where the dead bodies were found. During the 20s and 30s they extracted peat out there on a small industrial scale. They dug the peat, dried it, somehow dragged it out to the railway, and got it transported to customers. The Wild Moss is only about a kilometre away from Hällerum. I have seen photos today of people working with the harvest in Hällerum who we know lived in

Kirsta and worked on the peat bog. The work extracting peat must have been a special thing even then, and something that would have been of interest for your grandfather to document. I would be surprised if he never was there."

"That seems exactly as something he would have been attracted to. You should see some of his other stuff. He could really find odd people at odd places doing odd things. You mentioned Kirsta on the phone. I have looked for Kirsta in Granddad's notes but found nothing. Nothing for Wild Moss either, but that would hardly be the official name. There is no mention of Wild Moss on any map I have, but Kirsta is present on most maps from the 1930s. Could this peat bog have, or have had, another name?"

"If he had called it Hällerum Peat Bog or something similar, the photos should have been in the Hällerum binders. By the way, a thought just struck me: Östrahult? Östrahult is as a matter of fact closer to the Wild Moss than is Hällerum. Östrahult is however next to nothing, just four farms and two-three other houses. Östrahult Peat Bog? I have never heard that name, but there may of course have been folks in Östrahult preferring that name."

Anita lit up:

"I wonder, I wonder. I didn't know the geography out there well enough to understand that Östrahult was that close. I know there are a couple of binders labelled 'Östrahult'."

"All right," said Jan-Christer. "I understand you will return to digging in the basement. I hope first I may offer a Cognac to the coffee."

16

We found three thick binders labelled 'Östrahult 1928', 'Östrahult 1933', and 'Östrahult 1937', respectively. All three binders contained a subsection called 'Extracting peat from Östrahult Peat Bog"!

"My goodness! Anita! This is too good to be true."

There were in all at least 100 photos from the area I would call the Wild Moss. A superb documentation of how people worked to dig the peat, to dry it, to stack it, and to transport it out to the railway and load it on to carriages pulled by steam locomotives. Nils and Edvin Karlsson and Helvig Lindberg appeared on many photos, often together with young boys whose names I did not recognise. Probably seasonal workers. Torn and dirty clothes. Marked by poverty. Today this is called child labour.

In the binder from 1937 were two photos which almost made me fall off the chair. On the first of these photos are, as usual, a few boys or young men together with Nisse, Edvin and Helvig, but then there are two other adults, one man and one woman. The woman is with near certainty the same woman I saw on the photo from the harvest lunch earlier in the day. The presumed

Alvina. Here she is side by side with Helvig, the arms around each other's shoulders. The two equally tall, and taller than all others on the picture. The two very much alike. Who could she be if not Alvina? The second unknown person on the photo is a man leaning against a birch tree. He wears a slouch hat, and he has a handkerchief tied around his neck. He looks strong and robust but not fat. The three adult men on the photo — Nils, Edvin, and the unknown man — had very different body shape, but they had something in common in the facial features, something difficult to define clearly. This despite Nils having fatty and floppy cheeks which were the complete opposite to the others. Is this stranger a visitor from Minnesota? Is he the brother Vilhelm? On the backside of the photo a contour of the group was drawn with pencil. The names of all are given, except for those I believed could be Alvina and Vilhelm. Instead, it says for those two 'name not given'.

Once again, I scrutinised the photo from the lunch in my Grandparents' garden. Is the unknown man present on that photo too? Perhaps. On a chair, just in front of the presumed Alvina, sits a man. It could be him, but the photographer stood a bit too far away up on a slope for details to be clear. The photo shows 25 individuals, and uncovering details was not the purpose. Under the unknown man's chair is something that could be a hat, but one can't be sure. Maybe my romantic fantasy makes me dream up things, but doesn't Alvina hold her hand on the man's shoulder in a loving and intimate way? Something so completely against the severe and punishing Lutheran culture that plagued this part of the country so much 70–80 years ago. Fortunately, that culture has been uprooted and thrown out by now. That liberation process started with my generation not accepting the rigid nonsense. Maybe a professional image analysis can reveal more. I will ask if I can borrow the negative if it exists.

The other jaw-dropping photo from the binder labelled 'Östrahult 1937', showed only Helvig and the woman who must be Alvina. From just below the shoulders and up. They stood shoulder by shoulder. A fantastic photo. Black and white and all shades of grey. Here one can see that Helvig was somewhat haggard. Among other things she had lost one tooth in the upper jaw. Despite this she radiates an intense beauty and sensuality. Alvina looks as if she were on her way to the catwalk, or as if the photo were taken from a commercial for some beauty product. Uncompromised self-confidence. Like identical twins separated at birth, and one growing up in poverty and the other in a wealthy, happy and goodhearted banker's home. On the backside of the photo Kjell had written: 'The older woman is Helvig Lindberg. The younger does not want to disclose her name, but who can have any doubt that they are sisters?"

These two photos from the peat bog were both taken on 5th September 1937, two weeks after the lunch in my Grandparents' garden. Helvig would have been

45 and Alvina 39 years of age. In February 1938 Edvin sold Kirsta, the house as well as the land belonging to it, just half a year after these photos were shot. One wonders what happened out there on the Wild Moss during those six months?

All in all, I asked Anita for 20 photos to take with me. Two of these were chosen just out of personal interest. One was of myself, 4 years of age, standing at harvest time on an open field which I know so well with my maternal Grandfather, my special favourite. He was 58 on the occasion. He could not straighten one knee, and he had already by then a bad limp and probably pain. He never complained and never went to see a doctor. His hair still almost pitch-black, only a few hairs turned white as snow. Granddad had a scythe hanging seemingly carelessly over his shoulder.

The second private photo was of my parents from 1949, a year before I was born. They stand in front of a threshing machine in full action. Looking at the picture you get a feeling of hearing the deafening noise. The air is dusty, and the chaff is flying. This threshing machine is probably the one that for many years stood rusting behind my grandparents' cowshed, and which I used as a jungle gym during my childhood. The other 18 pictures were such I considered of value for my investigation.

"Great!" Anita said energetically, "I'll start working in the dark room right away. Quite a few things to do which I love. Early tomorrow morning paper copies will be dry and nice. I will make digital copies as well and load them onto a memory stick for you. I will be busy probably till about 1.00 a.m. Now you and Janne please relax with a glass of wine or whatever you want. It has been so nice to have you here Anders. Next time let's take the boat out on Hjälmaren. Nice fishing out there. See you at breakfast."

Before closing my eyes, a brief conversation with Saku… "Butterfly, it tickles! Return to my ankles, and then slowly back up to the shoulder. I will need a shower to cool down. Today I will book tickets my love. In about a week the tropical flower comes to the butterfly. Shouldn't it be the other way around? The butterfly is so good at crossing oceans."

17

The train journey from Stockholm Central Station up north to Sundsvall was calm and nice. I dozed for a while, but I also enjoyed a nice breakfast onboard. My thoughts circled around my tropical flower, but also around less pleasant matters.

I had learnt many things about Kirsta, about the peat extraction out in the Wild Moss, and about the people involved, from the photos in Anita's remarkable archive. Maybe the most startling discovery, beside the more emotional moments viewing photos of Helvig and Alvina, was the unknown man with the slouch hat and handkerchief who suddenly appeared in Kirsta and perhaps in Hällerum. Is it Vilhelm? Victim or perpetrator? Or neither? Did he have a romantic relation to Alvina? DNA analysis on Nisse's remains will soon reveal if Nisse and the murdered man were genetically closely related.

Results should come within a few days. Tonight, I must call Minnesota. Maybe Vilhelm was a well-known person over there. I will ask for an office in the Sundsvall Police HQ where I can sit and work for an hour or two tonight and maybe tomorrow morning also.

It is so much better to communicate on a landline than over a mobile. Usually better and more stable sound. Alvina? I must initiate work to get permission to open the grave where Alvina's parents lie. If they are parents to the murdered woman, then the identity is established. At the same time, I must not be carried away by my optimistic mind. All this still can be totally wrong. Maybe the victims have no relation whatsoever to Alvina and Vilhelm, or with the other folks in Kirsta. In a way that would be a relief. Should that be the case, I will recommend to Jan Norberg that we close this investigation.

The photos in Maja Kinnunen's collection could hardly bring important new knowledge to the case. Anita's photos were from the critical years just prior to when this horrible thing happened, while Maja Kinnunen's collection is much older, at least the part of it that contains shots of Helvig and Alvina. It will be emotional to see the girls as children. Maybe it was hasty to book a meeting with Maja. However, here I am in Sundsvall, and Maja has taken half a day off from work.

Just as I had exited the train in Sundsvall and was walking on the platform, my mobile rang. Calling was Åsa Svensson from Forensic Medicine.

"Hi Anders! Where are you?"

"I'm just off the train in Sundsvall. I will meet up with a relative of Alvina and Helvig Lindberg. The sisters' cousin's granddaughter. The leading theory is that it is Alvina Lindberg who is the murdered woman. This relative, Maja Kinnunen, has old family photos she has promised to show. When you call you always have important stuff to tell, and I know you never waste time on small talk during working hours. So, get on with it."

"Yes, I do believe this is interesting for you. Pia has worked hard, and now we have results from the DNA analysis of the remains from Nils Karlsson. The results are so interesting that I call you without awaiting the formal report. Nils Karlsson and the murdered man were close relatives. Brothers, with nearly full certainty!"

"Wow! I don't know should I be sad or happy. Now at least we know something."

"Yes. The likelihood this is a coincidence is virtually zero. That's how it is."

"Here is so noisy. I sit on a bench on the platform, and everyone around here seem to have decided to scream continuously. Can we talk more in a while?"

"Sure. I think you have grasped the essential part of it. We work on a report. It will be finished in two days."

18

The taxi took me through Sundsvall's most exclusive parts. Enormously large, all wooden, perfectly maintained old villas, many of them at least a hundred years old, side by side with modern architectural innovations. We stopped in front of an ultra-modern villa, surrounded by a beautiful wall made of granite. The house was nestled between high pines and birches, and the house itself looked as if a number of cubes of various sizes had been stacked beside and on top of each other in an irregular and random manner by a child. Between the cubes there were few, if any, right angles or level planes. Much glass and much concrete and stone. Impressive to say the least, though not precisely my preference. The entrance from the pavement was in a niche in the stone wall. Thirty metres to the left was a garage door. The garage seemed to be dimensioned for three cars standing side by side. I rang the bell.

"Good afternoon. Whom am I talking to?"

It was not Maja Kinnunen who spoke, but a lady with a hint of a southern accent and with a cultivated voice and language.

"Good afternoon. I am Chief Investigator Anders Andersson. I have a meeting booked with Mrs Maja Kinnunen for one o'clock."

"Mrs Kinnunen is expecting you. Welcome."

There was a clicking sound from the door which automatically opened smoothly. I walked on a path paved with stones to the entrance door in the nearest of the concrete cubes. A maid opened the door from inside when I was two metres away from it, and three metres into the hall stood Maja. I got a mild shock! Here was a copy of Helvig and Alvina! How breathtakingly amazing! Such strong genes! Tall and slim with a perfect figure. Long curly black hair interspersed with grey. The shape of the lips so much like Alvina's in particular. The hawk-shaped nose. I knew Maja was 52 years of age. Had I not known, I would have guessed 40–45.

"Good afternoon and welcome. I am Maja Kinnunen."

Maja spoke with a soft and slightly husky voice, slowly and in a cultivated and well-modulated manner. People interested in dialects, as I am, could hear traces of a northern intonation. As she came a few steps towards me and gave me her hand, she did so with a relaxed rhythm, and she radiated calm and a rock-solid self-assurance. She wore a comfortable, simple, red cotton dress reaching half calves, disclosing a marked but not thread-thin waist. She had beautiful strong ankles and attractive soft calves full of shape, sandal-like shoes with a slight heel. Toenails were red as red can be.

"Good morning. I'm Anders Andersson. Thank you for receiving me."

"Your errand seems important. The lack of knowledge about Helvig's and Alvina's fate is a heavy burden on the family. Not all of us have forgotten that they have existed. May I offer coffee, or whatever you prefer, before we view the photos?"

"Black coffee would be nice. I too have some photos I think will be of interest to you."

Maja instructed the maid in a language I did not understand, nor was I able to identify the language with certainty. Walking up a short flight of steps Maja said:

"You have researched the family so I'm sure you know I am Roma, or at least I have Roma roots. Many have said I have strong Roma features. I did not grow up with the language, but I have learnt elementary Romani at an adult age. Whenever possible we employ Romas for household work and for maintenance. Some reverse discrimination feels excusable."

After having ascended the short flight of steps, I was shown to a comfortable armchair in a small, cosy room with modern art in mainly warm colours hanging on the walls. After a few minutes, the maid came with coffee for me and tea for Maja, and a few biscuits.

"You have a remarkable and unique house!"

"Yes, Esa, my husband, studied architecture, which is his passion, before getting into management and economy. When we settled here in Sundsvall, and we got economy for it, this project he had always dreamt of became a reality."

After a while Maja lead the way until we arrived at something looking like a library. All walls were covered by shelves full of books, binders and boxes, everything meticulously clean and, as it seemed, well organized. On a table, which seemed rather to belong in a spaceship, in the middle of the room, stood a few binders.

"I understand you have most of the facts. Helvig, born 1892, and Alvina, born 1898, were first cousins of my maternal Grandfather. My Grandfather's uncle was their father. The girls' mother died 1909, and the two were left with an evil father totally lost in alcoholism. The girls disappeared 1910 and no one in the family ever heard of them."

"What a sad story! I have photos that will be of great interest to you. Not only happy news."

"My Granddad's father lived for 15 years after the girls had disappeared, and I have been told he was devastated and broken-down by the tragedy. He tried to find them but without success. He blamed himself throughout life for not doing enough to help the girls while that would have been possible. Some others blamed him too."

We went through the albums with family photos shot by Maja's Great Granddad. We were both moved. Tears ran down my cheeks, and even more so on Maja's.

Maja many times sobbed so that her body was shaking. Some photos were shot in a studio, and there the children were cute and clean sitting on the mother's lap. In the photos from day-to-day life the girls wore torn clothes, ill-fitting shoes, and they were more or less dirty. Worst of all was the thought of the life awaiting Helvig in particular. Helvig looked mature before her time, burdened by responsibility, while Alvina looked more like planning practical jokes.

I told what I knew about the bodies in the Wild Moss and about my memories of Helvig. Maja was totally perplexed and utterly moved by seeing the pictures of Helvig and Alvina shot by Kjell Johansson in the 1930s.

"My good Lord! Never ever could I dream of viewing photos of them as adults. This is of immense importance to me! Do you understand?"

When we came to the masterly portrait of the sisters standing shoulder to shoulder, then Maja burst into an unbridled wail.

"It's like it were me! My beloved! Thank you for showing this to me."

19

When Maja had recovered somewhat from the emotional shock, she invited me to stay for dinner, and even to stay overnight. I could use an office in the house during the evening to call Minnesota and for working with other matters. I accepted the offer and called my colleagues at the Sundsvall Police to inform them I would come to the police station Tuesday morning instead.

"Since I was home from work this afternoon, both maids have the evening off today. You will have to endure my cooking. I will serve oven-baked char-boiled potatoes with a white sauce based on sour crème, garlic and dill, and a green salad. Probably a soup to start with. I think Knorr powder fish soup is excellent, particularly if a few frozen prawns are added. An advantage is that it is made in five minutes. Usually, we refrain from any dessert. You are perfectly welcome to have a glass of wine. Esa and I never have wine on the evening before a working day. Just mineral water."

I connected my computer in a room high up and far back in the house. It was difficult to tell on which floor I was, but probably on fourth, or possibly somewhere between third and fourth. I had a view over the rear side of the house into the garden. I could not see where the garden ended. 'Garden' was perhaps not the correct word for it, rather it was like a large piece of land with a somewhat cultivated forest. My room was, like everything else in the house, modern and tastefully furnished. A large oil painting on canvas showing a landscape in yellow and shades of brown and an intensely blue sky with lovely complex clouds, hung on one wall. The artist had been inspired by both Cézanne and van Gogh.

I dialled the number to the County House of Freetown County up in northern Minnesota. After some time, a man with a somewhat drawly way of talking picked up the phone:

"Hello, Freetown County office. Nelson Brown speaking. What can I do for you?"

"Good morning. My name is Anders Andersson and I'm calling from Sweden. Is it possible for you to connect me to Mr Peter Karl?"

"Yes. I can see from here that he is in his office. I'll connect."

Peter Karl spoke much more energetically, and he sounded friendly. I introduced myself without disclosing I was from the police.

"Hi Anders, thanks for calling. Up here we have many Swedish descendants. I'm one of them. Maybe they liked it up here because here is as bitterly cold as where they came from. Probably worse. No, seriously, these are wonderful areas wintertime also. One just must have proper clothing. What can I do for you?"

"I want to ask about a person who emigrated from Sweden 1910 and who settled in Freetown County according to our sources. His name was Vilhelm Karlsson. I would like to know as much as possible about him. I can explain later why we are interested if you have time and if you would be interested. Do you have archives or some sort of sources where we could find information?"

A long silence followed. I thought the line had been cut, but then it was like Peter Karl took a deep breath and he started to talk.

"Oh yes, there are sources. You can start with me. Vilhelm Karlsson was my paternal Grandfather! He changed names in 1918 to Willie Karl. Willie Karl was most well-known up here.

Now it was my turn to become speechless for several seconds.

"But what on earth are you saying? Is it true? Are you really sure?"

"Guaranteed! We even have a small museum in this very house about the fate of Willie Karl and Alvina Lindberg. Unknown fate that is. Alvina Lindberg was Willie's partner and my paternal Grandmother. Do you know the name of this little township? Karlsville! It is not named after me."

"This is almost too much! Do you have time to talk?"

"I must appear in court in a few minutes. I earn my livelihood as a lawyer. Can we talk in about three hours? I will give you my direct number."

The dinner with Maja and Esa Kinnunen was simply delicious. I felt I needed a glass of Sauvignon Blanc. Esa Kinnunen did not give the impression one expects from the CEO of a major industrial conglomerate. He seemed reserved, almost shy. I observed many signals that Maja and Esa were intensely and warmly in love. Esa's foot repeatedly touched Maja's ankle and calf under the table. Maja's lips were sensually shaped when she met Esa's gaze. I heard, when they walked off to get coffee and tea, that they communicated in a language that I, with almost full certainty, identified as Finish.

"But Maja! Don't tell me you know Finish also! How much space is there in your brain?"

Maja laughed.

"My Finish is about on the same level as my Romani. I couldn't allow our kids and my husband to talk about me without me understanding."

"She understands every word. Some word endings are not correct when she speaks, but who cares?"

At coffee I updated Maja and Esa of the remarkable telephone conversation I had before dinner with Peter Karl, grandson of Alvina Lindberg and Vilhelm Karlsson. Maja was baffled, moved, and speechless. I said also I would travel over to Minnesota very soon to find out as much as possible about what could have happened to Willie and Alvina. This was nothing, in my opinion, which should burden Swedish taxpayers. It is not that type of police investigation. It has become my private passion. Maja said:

"Anders! May I come along? I can take a week off. It would be of immense importance to me. The family owe Helvig and Alvina so much. Let me cover all expenses! You understand we are very well off. Please!"

When I, later in the evening, called Peter Karl, then Maja sat by my side, and we had the loudspeakers on. Now I introduced myself as Chief Investigator from the Swedish Criminal Police, and Maja, Alvina's first cousin's grandchild, as representing the family in Sweden. I explained the case thoroughly. All facts and reasonable hypotheses. Peter largely stayed silent, though on several occasions we heard something sounding like gasps and once or twice, 'Oh my good Lord'. When I finished, Peter took over, calmly and methodically.

"What a horrible and sad story you have told me, and it explains a lot. I will try to relate what I have. Willie, let me call him so, seems to have arrived here to Freetown County in 1913. He would have been 20 years of age. Rapidly he became respected and held in high esteem by most. He had his enemies also; I will come back to that later. He worked hard and it seemed he knew how to do almost anything. He was also known to be a free spirit who did not appreciate it if people tried to teach him how to live and what to do. Towards folks who did not interfere and who minded their own business, he was friendly and reliable. He bought land and built a house about 40 kilometres from here out in pure wilderness. His land had border to one of the largest First Nations of the country. Willie got along well with the natives. They hunted together, and he was many times invited to their events.

We know he was in Sweden for most of 1917. In the year 1920 he told friends he was going to Sweden again, this time to bring a treasure with him back here. He came back eight months later. The treasure was Alvina. They seemed to have a good life. They prospered, and Alvina gave birth to two children. The two kids were named after Alvina's sister and Willie's brother in Sweden. My aunt Helvig was born 1924 and my father Edvin 1926. Helvig is still among us. She lives in an assisted living in Duluth and is in relatively good health. My father Edvin passed away last year.

Willie became a legendary trapper and a wholesaler of fur. That part of what he did would not have been allowed today, but those were different times. He also founded a construction company employing 30 workers, many of those were Native Americans. Willie and Alvina were by far the richest in the county. At the same time, they were highly controversial for many, and unconventional. For example, they were not religious and not married. Willie was hot tempered and blasted and chased away those who interfered in their lives. For more extreme religious groups Willie and Alvina became like a red curtain, as if they were sent by the devil. Also, the fact that they had good relations with the Natives was taken as a sign of their heathendom.

Then came *annus horribilis* 1936. A bank robbery in a neighbouring town derailed and two bank officers, a married couple, were shot dead. They left two small children. The robbers had facemasks obviously, but one was a white, strong male with long blond hair, and the other was a tall, slim woman with black, long hair. Several witnesses would lay their hand on the bible and swear Willie and Alvina were the robbers. Thinking analytically about it, people should have had doubts about this. Willie and Alvina were very wealthy and had no reason whatsoever to rob a bank. On top of that Willie had a rock-solid alibi, he had namely been out hunting for two whole days with a group of Natives. This alibi, however, infuriated certain groups even more. Protected by heathens! Blind, irrational hatred spread. A lynch-mob plundered and wrecked their home, and Willie, Alvina and the children had to flee for their lives.

It was said to have been a miracle they could escape at all. Nine days after robbery, the children were left with friends in Duluth. That was 9th of April 1936. Willie and Alvina disappeared, and no one has ever heard from them since. The children were adopted two years later by the family they had been left with, and they had a good life. The general belief was that 'justice', which in this case means the execution patrol, had caught Willie and Alvina and finished them off.

Not until 1946 was the truth about the bank robbery revealed. It would take a whole novel to explain everything, but as a side result of a major police investigation in Chicago, investigators found evidence that the bank robbery here in 1936 had been committed by a well-known gangster from Chicago and his Native American mistress. This obviously caused an enormous stir up here, and lots of soul-searching. However, Willie and Alvina remained missing, and the truth about their disappearance was never revealed. Their house was rebuilt, and a small museum about their lives and deeds was erected here in the County House. In 1960 they went so far as to change the name of this town from Freetown to Karlsville. I moved up here from Minneapolis 15 years ago since I find the quality of life here outstanding. Like a paradise for a guy with my personality."

The Kinnunens went to bed already at ten. I lay awake for two hours listening to Scarlatti and Handel's Concerto Grossi opus 3 with Neville Marriner and St Martin's in the Fields. It's twelve thirty, I can't call Saku now. I set the alarm for two thirty and fell into deep sleep.

"My butterfly spoils his flower when he calls in the middle of his night. I feel beautiful and attractive. Kiss me and climb on me."

I had to come out of the euphoria and inform Saku about recent events. I would have to go to the US in a couple of days and stay there for at least a week. I said nothing about Maja coming with me. Saku is not immune to jealousy, and I felt uncertain how she would react to me travelling alone with such an utterly attractive woman.

"My beloved, I understand. We could meet in New York? But no, it's such a mess. Let's spend our time in your forests and have meatballs and pizza instead. How I love it! Sometimes a curry. I postpone my journey and will come in two weeks or so. I love this longing. Here is no shortage of things to do. Sweet dreams my love."

20

Next morning, a Tuesday, I said goodbye to Maja and Esa as they left for work. Now Maja was dressed formally in blue-grey skirt and jacket and a white blouse. She was as taken from a fashion magazine for women in the career. The hair was elegantly coiffured. She was perfectly beautiful and full of style, and she looked ten years older than when I first saw her. Even like this, her wonderful figure, and the sensual shape of her lips, ankles, and calves, forced a sensitive person like me to take a deep breath.

"Bye for now Anders. I will have tickets booked today. On Saturday from Stockholm and back home on the following Sunday. You can ask Peter to book grizzly-safe hotels for us up there. You understand the importance of all this to me. Thanks for taking me with you."

Maja gave me a lovely, somewhat professional hug, and kisses on both cheeks, while she skilfully avoided her hair to get disorganised. I could not avoid thinking it was fortunate Saku did not see and hear this.

At the police station in Sundsvall, I met with some old friends and colleagues, and younger officers came to have a chat, and in some cases, it seemed, to seek advice. Sometimes I felt my reputation was a bit exaggerated, and that people expected too much from me. I consider myself a poor mentor. Too impatient. Usually, what I wanted to tell them was: 'Just go ahead with it! For God's sake!' I had limited time for chat, thus soon I escaped into an office and connected my computer. The main goal today was to seek, and get, approval for opening Alvina's and Helvig's parents' graves up in Sorsele, and to get someone from Forensic Medicine go up there to take necessary samples.

All this went unexpectedly smoothly. Six telephone calls around the country and a long email to the graveyard authority in Sorsele. Among others Hugo Lindberg gave his consent without any hesitation. The graveyard authority in Sorsele impressed me with their prompt action. Maybe they were not themselves aware of all regulations, but I said nothing. Everything practical would be done on Tuesday one week from now, thus results of DNA analyses should be available as Maja and I returned home from Minnesota.

After all these practical matters were set and decided, I simply sat for an hour in the office contemplating. There is little doubt that Vilhelm Karlsson, a.k.a. Willie Karl, was the man lying buried in the Wild Moss. The woman by his side was with all likelihood Alvina Lindberg, though so far, we only have circumstantial evidence for that. In a week and a half, we will have more hard facts about Alvina too. It seems so unlikely Willie lies there with another Roma woman but let's deal with that when and if such a riddle arises. So far so good. Now it seems overly optimistic to believe I can get much further in this investigation. Had the execution mob in Minnesota found out where Willie and Alvina were hiding, and sent a patrol over the ocean? Far-fetched, but the mob in Minnesota were blinded by hate, and they wanted, above everything else, to kill the couple thus commanding justice.

They were also convinced they had God on their side. And how on earth had Willie and Alvina otherwise been killed in this macabre manner? Like some sort of ritual. Had their unconventional way of living infuriated local Swedish extremist groups? Even more far-fetched. Certainly, Willie and Alvina's way of living, if it had become widely known, would have been seen with suspicion and disgust here too, but going so far as to an execution was simply not in the toolkit of locals. The temperaments here in Scandinavia are relatively mild, even in those with severely distorted minds and norms. It is difficult for me to see that local forces would have been capable and competent to do a thing like this. We will see. It's as simple as that.

Now I will go home to my house in Hällerum and walk in the forests, in the Wild Moss and other places that are just as special, enjoy music, have chats with Saku, and meet up with Mama a few times. Often, I plan days ahead which music I will listen to. Now I had Schubert's string quintet in mind, particularly the amazing recording with the Emerson Quartet supplemented with Rostropovich. Thereafter stir up the mind with something by Shostakovich. Maybe some of his string quartets with the fantastic Oistrakh Quartet? The remarkable version on YouTube where they play the third movement from the third quartet? Perhaps already now the capercaillie cocks are courting their hens in the deep woods and out in the Wild Moss at dawn. Still, it is a bit early in the year for that, but on the other hand we have had very mild weather, so, maybe after all they have started. For a moment, in my dream world, I asked myself whether Shostakovich ever might have had the opportunity to listen to a capercaillie cock courting his chosen hen. That might have inspired him to some of his remarkable compositions. Bach, on the other hand, probably would have seen the capercaillie love song as a primitive, perhaps disturbing, expression of an uncultivated nature. Jimi Hendrix would have been excited and delighted.

21

In the arrival hall at the Duluth Airport stood a taxi driver with a sign 'Kinnunen Andersson'. The agreement was we would rest in the hotel and meet Peter Karl on the next day, a Sunday. He would pick us up at the hotel at 9.00 a.m. and take us to Alvina and Willie's daughter Helvig, now 93. After that we would drive up to Karlsville, a journey of about four hours.

Maja had booked business class flight tickets; thus, we had restful and comfortable flights Stockholm-Chicago-Duluth. I felt an enormous relief when Maja, after a long silence, mid-air over the Atlantic, said:

"Anders, maybe I make a fool of myself saying the following, but on the other hand a lack of fearfulness is probably what has taken me to where I am. What I want to say to you is that we shall not get into any romantic adventures you and I, although I feel there is strong attraction between us. I have an exceptional marriage with Esa. I feel like the most privileged woman on earth, and you have such a strong relationship with Saku. If we go beyond the borders, it will be seen on us as clearly as if it were written in capital letters on our foreheads. I like you so much. A pleasant tension in the body. Do you feel like I do?"

"Yes Maja, I could never have said it better. I feel the forces, and I'm utterly relieved by what you said. No romantic adventures."

Shortly after 9.30 Sunday morning, as we sat with coffee and tea after a light breakfast in the hotel restaurant, we saw a man entering the room. He looked around, saw us, and came right up to us.

"Good morning, Maja. I'm Peter Karl, your third cousin. I do assume you are Maja Kinnunen?"

"Oh yes! Hi Peter! How could you be so sure I was the one?"

"Photos I've seen of my grandmother, plus features of my Auntie Helvig whom you will meet today. Simply an amazing similarity in appearance! No doubt whatsoever! Somehow there are exceptionally strong female genes in the family, although that might be an unscientific way to put it. You will meet more relatives up here who look so much like Grandma and auntie Helvig. And so much like you."

Peter seemed just as nice and open-minded as he had sounded on the telephone. His looks were Scandinavian, except for the deeply brown eyes, which made the overall impression more multifaceted. He was of medium height, seemed strong and in excellent physical condition. The hands could have belonged to a lumberjack; thus, he probably did not spend all his time in the County Office or in the Court room. Maja and

Peter hugged each other, visibly struck by emotion. When we shook hands, the grip was steadfast and powerful to the extent that my long, lean, and relatively weak hand was paining. Maja asked a question she and I had discussed:

"Peter, we have told you we bring photos showing Alvina and her sister Helvig both as children, but also as adults after Alvina came back to Sweden. Alvina and Willie would have come to Sweden 1936, but the photos are from 1937. On two photos we believe Willie appears, but there is no one in Sweden, to our knowledge, who can identify him. Maybe your auntie Helvig can identify her father, she was 12 as he disappeared. Will it be too emotional? We don't want to create disturbance in her mind. Should we tell her we suspect her parents were murdered?"

"Auntie Helvig is at least as clear-minded as I am. I have told her about the bodies buried in the peat bog and about your suspicions. Show her the photos. Of course, it will be emotional, maybe she will shed tears, but she will get over that part. Later we will view lots of photos up in Freetown County. The identification of Willie, or the opposite, will not pose any problem. Auntie Helvig would become angry if you don't show her everything and if you don't talk to her as to an adult. She is totally aware of her history. The couple who adopted her and my dad were the best friends of Alvina and Willie, and they were amazing people. Helvig and my dad were lucky and got a very good life given the circumstances. Perhaps I should prepare you by saying that my aunt is not a silent and restrained person. For example, she is a convinced atheist, and she hates Christian hypocrisy. She does not keep these views a secret. Probably she is much like her father Willie in temperament and in the outlook on life. Most likely Helvig's daughter Anna will be with her today as we come. Maja, you may not know it, but the family here in Minnesota has been productive. Willie and Alvina had only two kids, but those two kids had five children each. Thus, you have ten third cousins in this country. Eight of them live in this region. I have counted 33 children of your third cousins."

"Oh! I knew nothing about that. So, we will start with Helvig. She seems to be a lady who knows what she wants. Give me ten minutes to change to something better."

"You look fantastic as you are but take ten minutes if you so wish. I could add that Helvig knows some Swedish. I can't judge how good that Swedish is. Until she was 12, they spoke mainly Swedish at home. Later she has been a member of a Swedish club here in Duluth. The interest in language and traditions of the forefathers is growing in the country. There are evening courses in Swedish and other 'Old World' languages available in Duluth, and some from the younger generations also take part."

22

Meeting Alvina's 93-year-old daughter Helvig was refreshing, intense, and moving, all at the same time. She came towards Maja with astonishingly smooth and effortless steps, arms lifted as if prepared for a hug. She halted two metres from Maja, saying in broken but fully understandable Swedish:

"But dear! It is as if I saw Mama! I simply can't believe it!"

We thought the same of Helvig. Tall and lean, with age somewhat skinny and bony, the shoulders probably not as broad as they once were, but the overall posture still straight. The hair was thick and grey with streaks of pitch-black refusing to give in. The face shared many of Alvina's and the Swedish Helvig's features. She looked precisely as one would have imagined Alvina, had she been allowed to reach this age. The daughter Anna was blond and chubby but had the same easy-going and uncomplicated mindset. We talked, watched photos, had coffee and cookies. I told my story about the findings in the Wild Moss. Helvig was moved seeing many of Maja's photos, and angry and shaken when hearing what I said, but she was a tough lady. Her dearest possession was a photo of Mama Alvina and Aunt Helvig as children. This photo must have its origin in the same collection as the one Maja had taken care of. Maja has several, nearly identical photos. Helvig serious, as if burdened by responsibility, about 15 years of age, and Alvina about 10 looking as if she was planning to crack a joke. It was confirmed that the man we had presumed to be Vilhelm Karlsson, indeed was Willie Karl. "Oh yes, Mama and Papa. My most beloved!" As we came to the portrait of Alvina and Helvig, standing shoulder by shoulder out in the Wild Moss, then Helvig, and Maja too, burst into uncontrollable tears. Helvig's skinny body shook, and tears flooded her face.

"My wonderful Aunt Helvig! Why did they not allow you to come to us? Mama always said Aunt Helvig in Sweden was the kindest person in the whole world, and that she one day would help her to come over to us. Had not the idiotic, evil devils killed them, Mum and Dad would have brought Helvig here to us. They would all have come back to us. Look how happy Mama was when she was with Helvig!"

I was of course struck by Helvig's words. Thus, I asked:

"So, Helvig, who do you believe killed your parents?"

"Now I know they managed to get to Sweden, so maybe I shouldn't be so sure any longer. Up until now I have been totally convinced that the evil beast Larry

Swenson and his mob caught them somewhere in this country and killed them."

"But they may have followed them all the way to Sweden. That is by no means impossible."

"I would not be surprised. A worse hellish bastard has never existed."

"Can you tell me about Larry Swenson. Who was he?"

"He was a lumberjack; enormously big and strong they say. He was a master to handle the axe, and he competed in lumberjacking around the country. It is said he was one of the best there ever was. He won the Minnesota championship, and he also became Wisconsin champion. How he could become Wisconsin champion is difficult to explain since he came from Minnesota, but he must have cheated with his identity. Not unexpected because he always cheated in everything. When he was 44–45 years, he claimed to have met Jesus in the woods. Jesus himself had told Larry he was his selected prophet. What rubbish! Larry bragged about his encounter. I suppose he was fed up with logging. Some uneducated poor people actually believed him! He started to preach about God and the Devil in an extreme way, and silly fools joined his church. He also fooled them to believe God wanted them to give money to the church. Larry Swenson became filthy rich. He hated Mum and Dad. He said they lived in sin like heathens, probably sent by the Devil. He turned people against us. They say that on some Sundays he preached only about what a horrible man my Dad was. One must also feel some pity for Larry. He was in the bank when it was robbed, and it was his brother and sister-in-law who were killed. He was fully convinced my parents were the robbers, and he swore to God to take revenge."

Just before we were to leave, Helvig said:

"There is one more thing I want you to see Maja, and you Anders may of course also read it. Anna and Peter will not understand because it is in Swedish."

Helvig took an old envelop out from a chiffonier, and she pulled a sheet of paper out of the envelope with utmost care. It was a letter from Helvig in Sweden to Alvina in Minnesota, dated 5th of April 1932. We read the letter, and tears were impossible to hold back. It was a long letter. Helvig had a beautiful handwriting, and she had a mastery of the language. Thinking about the life she had, the letter was immensely impressive. Here follow a few excerpts I found of interest for the investigation:

"Dear sister! Thank you for your letters. I am happy you are fine, that the children are doing well, and that Vilhelm is nice to you. It seems I cannot get myself together to write more than one letter each year."

"Here in Kirsta and out on Östrahult Peat Bog, life is not easy. We work hard but do not earn much. Nils' and my extra income from working for the nice family in Hällerum saves us."

"Today we went to the shops in both Hällerum and Vibo to buy essentials. The shop in Hällerum has less and less to offer. Not many people go there any more. I fear it will soon close."

"Edvin is a hungry man, and I feel he loves me. We are intimate at least twice a week. It seems I cannot have children, or Edvin can't. Maybe that is a good thing. Our children would grow up in poverty."

"Yes Alvina, my beloved sister, how I would love to come over to you! We will see how that goes."

Tears were shed and we had difficulties to talk. I was also overwhelmed by bad conscience and disgust for my own behaviour. Twenty-three years after this letter was written, I was mean and condescending towards Helvig at a time when she needed help and respect more than ever. After a minute, I managed to say:

"Helvig! What a wonderful letter. Is this the only one you have? It sounds as if Helvig had written more letters to your mother."

"This is the only letter I have. There were many more, but in the chaos when we had to flee, this was the only one Mama managed to take with her. The others are gone, burnt, or they were stolen."

Those who plundered Willie and Alvina's home in 1936 possibly got access to information showing where it was most likely to find the couple in case they would be able to get to Sweden. Perhaps some hypotheses are not so far-fetched any longer.

23

The week in Minnesota was intense. Maja was invited to relatives every day. Some days she had two invitations, one day she visited three families. I accompanied her sometimes but usually not.

The museum devoted to Willie and Alvina was housed in two small rooms in the County Centre. On display were photos, weapons, and all sorts of objects the couple had left behind. Photos of Willie in front of large heaps of fur, gigantic moose horns, construction projects surrounded by workers. Wille and Alvina with the children in their home, with friends, visits by Natives, and visits to Natives' events. Alvina was good looking to say the least, and she seemed satisfied with life. She also looked as if filled with self-assurance. Willie, the man by her side, was strong and powerful, but Alvina was his independent equal. Lawrence Swenson and his church, or the conflict after the bank robbery, were not mentioned anywhere. Peter Karl explained:

"Being bitter enemies is not illegal. If anything were to be implicated, we could easily be sued. Helvig's reasoning wouldn't survive for long in court."

"Obviously I agree. I would, however, want to talk to someone who today is responsible for that church. There might be documentation of interest."

"The church still exists, and now Larry's grandson Christoffer Swenson is senior pastor. Christoffer is more of a mainstream pastor. He is much liked, and he does not scare the guts out of people nearly as much as did his grandfather. The church is in a town about 25 kilometres away from here. You can borrow one of my cars. Unfortunately, I'm expected in court in half an hour. I have met Chris a few times, but never debated the conflict between his grandfather and my grandparents. It is a bit far back in time. I'll call him to check if he is at home."

Christoffer Swenson was a big man in his fifties. The hair was reddish, and the skin was fair. He gave a pleasant impression, and he had black soil under his nails.

"Welcome! God bless! As I'm sure you understand I have Swedish ancestors. Our forefathers came to New York in 1848 and settled first just north of Duluth, and two years later they came all the way up here. Then it was even more of a wilderness than it is today. It is remote enough today, but then it was indeed an outpost facing untamed eternity. Untamed by white people that is. Natives have lived up here for hundreds, if not thousands, of years. My ancestors lived quite isolated up here, and for at least two generations they spoke more Swedish than English at home. They say my grandfather Larry was most comfortable in Swedish, and when he became exalted and rapturous during a service, many times he slipped over to Swedish without himself noticing. He grew up partly with his paternal grandparents, and they spoke only Swedish at home."

When I explained the reason for me coming, he grunted a bit, but he was not dismissive.

"Yes, my grandfather is said to have been an extremist. He died, or rather he disappeared, before I was born. His reputation is not the best. I know he swore to God to kill Peter Karl's paternal grandparents since he was convinced they had murdered his brother and sister-in-law and made two children orphans. Further, he thought Mr and Mrs Karl lived as heathens. There was fury around here after the bank robbery, and the Karls had to flee for their lives. They left the children with friends in Duluth and were never seen again.

Many believed my granddad and a mob had caught them and killed them. Ten years later it was revealed that Willie and Alvina were totally innocent of the bank robbery. It is said my granddad went into depression and seclusion when he realised the truth. Two years further on he simply disappeared, and he was never found. The general belief is that he took his own life somewhere out in the wilderness, but no one knows. I really don't know why all these bad things happened. It does not look good for my granddad, although there is no evidence for anything. Sure, you are welcome to go through the diaries and other things we have. I don't want to hide anything. Here are diaries covering activities from the day the church was founded by my granddad Lawrence in 1925. The pastor in charge has always documented things like number of attendees on Sundays, a brief summary of the sermon, and other things of interest whatever they may be. The total amount of offering was also always noted. My granddad, my dad, and I for that matter, have always been very dutiful with these matters."

"Thank you! I appreciate you being so helpful. Did your grandfather or your father leave personal diaries or other documents that might be of interest?"

"I don't think so. I have not seen other diaries. We have very few other documents of any kind. Other than those dealing legally with the property."

I sat in the church office for three hours, and it was time well spent to say the least. The diaries were well organised, date and name of acting pastor at the top, and a signature at the bottom of the page. One page for each Sunday. Sometimes the page was filled with text, sometimes there were only a few words. The structure made it easy to get an overview, and easy to go through the material. I commenced with the book starting in August 1934. With few exceptions Larry Swenson was the pastor on duty. On several occasions, Willie and Alvina were mentioned in the minutes as examples of errant people who will burn in hell. They live in sin, socialize with heathens, and are heathens themselves.

The bank robbery during which Larry's brother and sister-in-law were killed, took place on 31st of March 1936. No records were available in the church diary from the first four Sundays of April that year. On the 30th of April Larry was back with a preaching full of sorrow, but also with burning hatred and accusations towards Willie and Alvina, promises to take revenge on them. The police were accused of incompetence. Further, the preaching was replete with hatred towards heathens, probably referring to Natives, for protecting the ruthless killers.

Larry continued, with few exceptions, to write in the church diary each Sunday during the whole of 1936. The words steamed of fury and hatred. Then, halfway into January 1937, Larry ceased to be the pastor in office. Instead, a certain Joshua Seestrom took over. Seestrom always wrote 'Deputy for pastor Lawrence Swenson' under his own name on top of the page. Not until exactly one year later, mid-January 1938, did Larry return. Now he gave an astonishingly mild testimony, full of thankfulness to the Allmighty for the justice in his creation. I talked to Christoffer, and he knew of Joshua Seestrom.

"He was a hundred years old when he died. He was sort of a 'free-lance pastor'. As far as I know he did not have a congregation of his own, but he travelled around and served where needed. Reputation says he was a kind man. Demanding, but at the same time emphasizing the forgiving side of Christianity. They said he influenced my father, in his own mild way, to revolt against my granddad."

Christoffer was unaware that Josha Seestrom had deputized for his granddad during the entire 1937. Chris had no clue what Larry might have done during that year.

"Thanks for this, Anders. My father never said anything about it, and I have not read these diaries myself except for a few pages here and there. To be honest I have never been particularly interested."

I continued patiently to study Joshua's notes, Sunday after Sunday. His handwriting was nearly unreadable. Pages were cluttered, and apparent logic difficult to discern. A huge difference to the simple and clear notes by Pastor Swenson. My patience and perseverance were pushed to its limits, but suddenly I came across something astonishing an of greatest importance. In the notes from 14th of August, I read the following: '*I read to the congregation a letter sent to us by pastor Lawrence from Wexiö. There he had met likeminded, and he preaches the word of God. He sends his best regards and blessings to the Godly congregation in Minnesota.*"

My stubbornness! Thank you! Wexiö! Today the name is Växjö. The metropole in central southern Sweden. In 1937 one could travel by train from Växjö to the Wild Moss with only one change of trains. A thought struck: Passport! Expired passports are something people tend to keep. I asked Christoffer first about letters from pastor Lawrence to the congregation or to Joshua Seestrom:

"No, I have not seen any such letters. I'm almost sure nothing of that sort exists. I have gone through most old things not so long ago. If such letters ever existed, Joshua probably kept them. We should not be too optimistic ever to find those items. He was poor and lonely as an old man."

"Do you happen to have some old passports from your granddad lying around?"

"I do wonder. I think there is one. One tends to save expired passports. I hope no one else has gotten rid of it. I will go through a few drawers. Have another cup of coffee in the meanwhile."

Chris returned after fifteen minutes. In his hand, which looked like the hand of a hard-working farmer, he had an old passport. It was the passport of Lawrence Karl Swenson issued in Duluth on the 16th of December 1936. I didn't have to search for long. On the second page was a big and clear stamp showing Lawrence had entered Sweden in Gothenburg on 21st of March 1937, and on the third page a stamp showing he had exited from Gothenburg on 12th of December that same year.

24

Back in my room at the hotel in Karlsville I connected my computer to the WiFi. Mail from Åsa Svensson at Forensic Medicine in Linköping.

"Hi Anders! I hope all is well with you over there. Pia has been effective in the lab. The following probably does not come as a surprise: DNA-analyses show that Sofia and Johan Lindberg, buried in Sorsele, were parents of the woman who had been murdered and buried in the Wild Moss (as you call it). I can say this with full certainty. We look forward to meeting you next time you pass by. Åsa"

OK. Now this goes like an automatic piano playing a ragtime. Am I done with this investigation? It is clear, beyond reasonable doubt, that Alvina Lindberg and Willie Karl are the victims. Strong circumstantial evidence points at Pastor Lawrence Swenson as the leading perpetrator. Nothing that would hold for convicting Swenson in court, but in this case, there will be no court proceedings. All involved are long gone. However, it is difficult to imagine Lawrence Swenson did this alone. Willie was an extraordinarily strong and fit man used to handling weapons of all kinds. Probably he had access to guns, knives, axes etcetera when he was in Kirsta, and he was fully aware that pastor Swenson's highest desire was to kill, or massacre, him and Alvina. Willie would not give in easily, and he would have reacted violently at the sight of the pastor would he show up in Kirsta or out on the Wild Moss. However, on the dead bodies there were no signs whatsoever of any struggle before the executions. The only signs on Willie as well as Alvina were the cloven skulls and the injured vertebrae. Identical on both, with surgical precision. Was Lawrence disguised so that Willie and Alvina were fooled into some evil trap? Did Lawrence bring helpers from Minnesota so that Willie and Alvina could be somehow immobilized prior to a horrific ritual execution? Did he manage to recruit a mob in Sweden? Apparently, he preached in Växjö, thus possibly he could have brainwashed people there to help him fight the Devil.

Maja and I had an early dinner at the hotel, and we wished each other good night already shortly after eight. Maja would have coffee later in the evening with a family in Karlsville, and I looked forward to a calm and restful evening in my room. Maybe Requiem by Fauré and Raua Needmine by Tormis, the latter perhaps not so restful to listen to. The opening choral from Bach's St John's Passion with Richter and Münchener Bach-Chor and Münchener Bach-Orchester, and the final choral from the same recording. And Saku of course. Eleven and a half hours, thus why not try WhatsApp immediately? As far as I know she is back in Colombo, but she can of course already be out on town.

"My most beloved! Now I have tickets! I'll arrive in Copenhagen next Friday 11.30 a.m. Then you must be at home, and hopefully you can meet me at the airport. I long for the touch of your hands!"

"My Saku! I will be ready for you."

"There's so much here now. Probably I can stay for only two weeks, so I keep the return flight open. It so happens I am right now enjoying tea at Tea Breeze at the Racecourse Mall. Right beside me sit such a nice Swedish couple. I have bragged about you. I long for you. Is it healthy to be so much in love at our age? What do you think?"

"Yes my dearest Saku! I'm sure it's the best that can happen. Particularly when there is more spice than sugar. You are like chili mixed into Jaffna curry. I will meet you in Copenhagen. I love you!"

"How wonderful, my butterfly is so childish. I will look stunning when I come. My hair is so nice. I have found shoes that make my ankles look better than ever. You will love to touch me. You will become dizzy seeing me. I have already decided what to wear."

25

Saturday afternoon, the day before we started the journey back home, a barbeque party was arranged in Karlsville to celebrate and honour Maja. Sixty-three persons took part. Helvig was the oldest, the youngest was three months old. Maja gave a beautiful speech about the Swedish part of the family. The way she talked about the unpleasant reasons that had taken us to Karlsville was moving, honest, and in good taste. Maja spoke remarkably good English. Grammatically immaculate, British intonation, but not at all snobbish. Her vocabulary was astonishingly advanced. Not until I complimented her for her language skill in the plane on the way back home, did she reveal that she and Esa had lived in London for seven years before the three children were born. Then Maja had worked for an American investment bank.

"A stressful life. I can't tell you how much I appreciate life in Sundsvall. Talk about quality of life. I don't long for London or New York. Or for Stockholm for that matter."

Esa met Maja in the arrival hall at Arlanda Airport in Stockholm when we arrived Monday just after noon. They kissed devotedly, and Maja pressed her knee against Esa's thigh. It looks wonderful. That man has won the first prize in the lottery of life, and probably so has she. Such an exceptionally sensual and competent woman who always gets precisely what she wants.

I picked up my old Volvo at Jan Norberg's home in Stockholm, and then drove towards home in Hällerum after only a coffee with Jan's wife Greta. I also borrowed the landline telephone, and I succeeded to book a meeting at 11 a.m. on Wednesday with Sivert Svensson, a police colleague and particularly good friend in Växjö. After an excellent dinner at a roadside restaurant in Stavsjö, I arrived at my home in Hällerum at nine Monday evening.

On Tuesday I slept late, and I had a lunch with Mama. In the afternoon I had one of my favourite walks, involving crossing the Wild Moss, but I avoided coming in immediate vicinity of the burial site. Enough of that for now. I had a long walk, three and a half hours. Weather was mild, it felt like spring, and one would not have been surprised to hear the rattling bugle calls of a crane, though that would have been about six weeks early according to the calendar. Cranes are usually quite punctual in their migration. Plenty of capercaillies at the expected locations. The cocks took off with a deafening roaring noise when they felt I came too close. The sound of them taking off could scare the daylights out of an unprepared and ignorant wanderer.

Late in the evening I enjoyed the album Chops with Joe Pass and Niels Henning Örstedt Pedersen. Loud volume on my superb HiFi. I disturb none other than possibly moose walking by. At one of my first visits to London, in my mid-twenties, I managed to get a ticket to Ronnie Scott's on Frith Street in Soho, the famous jazz club I had read so much about. I was unaware of that on that particular evening, Joe Pass and NHÖP, these two giants of modern jazz, performed music that soon would be released on the album *Chops*. The room was packed, I was late, and there was no place for me to sit other than on the floor less than two metres away from Niels Henning's bass. Had I stretched my arm and leaned forward slightly, I could have touched the instrument. Such were the lack of rules those days. Life-changing coincidences.

26

Precisely at eleven on Wednesday morning I knocked on Sivert Svensson's open door in the police HQ in Växjö.

"Old man, hello! What a pleasure. Long-time no see! How are you?"

"Hi Sivert! I'm fine. As a matter of fact, better now than for some time. And you! You don't look a day older than last time we met. It must have been eight, if not ten, years ago."

"I'm OK. One should not complain. I do spend much time both in the gym and out walking in nature. I'm healthy and in good physical condition. But you know, I have some difficulties to get over a certain melancholy."

Sivert Svensson was 66, and the normal retirement age was 65. He wanted to work on overtime however, simply because he thought life would be too boring otherwise. He had not recovered mentally after his wife passed away unexpectedly seven years earlier. It had been impossible for me to attend the funeral due to a highly sensitive case, something that had bothered me deeply. Sivert's marriage had been full of warmth, but the couple had no children, something they had desired more than anything else. They had not managed to come to a decision to adopt a child before it was too late. They would have been wonderful parents. Sivert was a genuinely loyal and trustworthy colleague and friend, and about 20 years ago we had worked together on a complicated case. Now I had come to Växjö to visit Sivert due to old friendship, but also because he had lived and worked in Växjö all his life. He was the type of police officer who knew everybody, everybody liked him and had confidence in him, and he was passionately interested in local history and the local society. If there were one person now living who could help me dig into events that occurred in Växjö in the year 1937, it would be Sivert Svensson. I told Sivert my story in some detail.

"Well, well. That's something. You never surrender. You are doing the right thing. A sad story. How can I help you with this? These independent churches are nothing close to me. I'm a convinced atheist."

"I'm rather an agnostic. A human brain can never fully understand the universe. Even Einstein said so. So, what can one call the basic laws of universe and of the human mind? Some choose to call these fundamental laws the Will of God and they are free to do so. I don't believe, however, that anyone can pray to a God he believes exists, and thereby influence events."

"For me football and ice hockey are enough. But of course, I have contact also with many of those claiming to communicate vertically. I know almost everyone in this town."

"I thank you in advance for your support. I work on this case as a private detective, supported by my pension. What drives me is first of all the gruesome fate of Helvig. I'm so sad over how life treated her. She was probably a wonderful and smart person, but throughout life she was unfortunate and underprivileged. Here in Växjö I assume there were and are many independent, sometimes extreme, Christian congregations."

"We still have enough of them, though probably there were even more in the 1930s. I will call Pastor Ulf Löfgren. He is quite all right, and probably he knows more than anyone about that part of our local history. The nice thing is that he also is passionate about football, and that's how I know him. We have been board members of Växjö's major football club for years. When our team does something bad, he can become upset and even say dirty words. I know because I've sat next to him many times. He's a nice guy, and I have known him for decades. He is around 75, but totally clear-minded. His father was also a Pastor."

Ulf Löfgren was a small, thin, intense, weasel-like man. Totally bald. He received us in his home, a nice one-bedroom apartment in the centre of Växjö. He had moved here from a villa when his wife had died nine years ago. The apartment was, to my taste, overloaded with old furniture in dark wood. Photos covered almost every inch of the walls and stood on most available surfaces. Lots of family photos, photos from sermons in different churches, but just as much a plethora of photos of his favourite football team and many of its stars.

"Welcome. God bless! Sivert, how nice to see you again. Pre-season games are not so far away. I don't think we will do very well this year. Many of our youngsters are promising, but they need two-three years more to mature. But when they have matured, they probably move on to clubs with more money. That's how it is these days. Not nice, but who can blame the guys? Money rules the world. Investigator! I wonder what has brought you here. Obviously, I will assist you if I can. Law and order are dear to me. Please sit down on the sofa. I'll make coffee and then we can talk. My whole day is free of duties."

I introduced myself in more detail, and again I carefully walked through the story. Ulf Löfgren was fully alert. He sat on an uncomfortable chair with his back fully straight without leaning back. His hands in the lap.

"My dear what a mess. A horrible story! And now you want to know if I might know anything about some mad Swedish-American pastor visiting Växjö in 1937 who preached about hell and punishment."

"He himself writes in the letter he has been here, and that he had met with 'like-minded', so let's assume what he says is correct. I would like to know as much as possible about what happened here. Whom he might have met and so on. I know it was before your time.

However, maybe you heard stories being told when you grew up. Or you might be able to advise me where to look for information? Did the churches have diaries as in Minnesota? Anything. I feel a responsibility towards the memory of the victims to search for the truth as far as possible."

"Even before my time! I was born 1942, and this would have happened 1937. Well, at that time mammoths roamed the forests around here. No, seriously. It should be possible to find at least something. Most churches do have diaries like those you described from the US. Maybe not so detailed in most cases. It depends on the individual Pastor. Some do this ambitiously; others are less meticulous."

"If you could give me some hint where I could start searching, I would be most grateful."

"We do have some bad luck because my dad was placed way up north 1936 and 1937. Another problem is that there were so many churches in this region. One of the most extreme was named, 'Sin and Punishment'. It was no secret that active Nazis were drawn to that congregation. However, the same can be said of a few other churches also at that time. Not only churches. The society was infested with such sympathizers during the 1930s. All who are honest about our history know that. The Christian Non-Conformist Churches were probably not the worst. 'Sin and Punishment' was disbanded towards the end of the 1940s. That church had a particularly dubious reputation. It is likely that diaries and other compromising documents were destroyed after the war and after all the horrible revelations. Now, we do not know if Pastor Swenson had such sympathies. Maybe he was just an unusually dogmatic Pastor emphasizing the Devil's part of the biblical story more than most of us do. There were many other congregations too where possibly a strict and extreme American could have preached, particularly since this one could preach in Swedish. I can't remember my father ever mentioning anything about an angry American Pastor. Well, it is difficult to be more concrete. How else can I help you?"

"What about the local press in those days? Didn't they cover activities of the churches?"

Pastor Löfgren flipped his fingers and started to talk in a high-pitched voice:

"Wow! Now one understands that you are a Criminal Investigator! A splendid idea! Go to the town library, just across the street from here, and ask for Växjö Daily for the time period you want to study. That paper came three days a week; Monday, Wednesday, and Saturday. It was called Daily anyway because that was how it started early 20th century. It was in existence as late as into the 1980s. The owner was an immensely rich and religious landowner and his heirs. He was an industrialist and had sawmills and paper factories also. Växjö Daily covered church matters in the tiniest detail. The whole mid-section was devoted to such. Usually there were many nice photos also. Why didn't I think of that myself right away? It's the best you can do. I will think about what more I can do for you."

Sivert chipped in:

"I'll call the library now so they can collect the papers for tomorrow. Papers this old are probably buried deep in their archives, but they should be there. It may take some time to dig them out. Best if you start on that tomorrow. I know the folks there very well. They will fix it."

Sivert offered me to stay overnight using the bed-settee in the living room. I said no thanks but invited him for a dinner in town. Late evening and night, I simply wanted to spend by myself, with Saku, and with music. A small but excellent room in the Town Hotel was surprisingly cheap. I listened to Sokolov playing Mozart and Beethoven. Partly the same repertoire Saku and I had heard him play in Gulbenkian Main Auditorium in Lisbon just last year. Then a sharp change to Pollini and Chopin's nocturnes 1, 7, 8, and 13. Contrasts, but it is the same instrument.

"I'm done packing. Will not take much. I scrutinize myself in the mirror without anything on. I visit the gym whenever I can. My figure is excellent. I think you will be exalted when you see me. I hope so and I want it. I want to be the most beautiful flower for my butterfly."

My beautiful, childlike flower so filled with vanity, who, all of a sudden, can transform into a spitting cobra. At 25, living in Zürich, she was betrayed by a man she was deeply in love with. She resigned from a well-paid position at an insurance company, took a month off, and then took up a challenging job at a leading commercial bank in Paris. She stayed with the bank for 22 years. She became a cool and utterly professional economist, with total focus on work. She made a brilliant career, and when she was offered a top job at the bank's North American branch, she felt she had to make a choice. Instead of moving across the Atlantic, she handed in her resignation and moved back to Sri Lanka.

When she retired and moved back, the reason was not that she loved her old life in her country of birth. As much as she loved her country and its friendly, simple people, as much did she detest the arrogant ultra-rich social class to which she herself belonged. Envy, gossip, keeping wealth within a narrow group of people, the deeply rooted culture of not sharing with the less fortunate, and finding more or less ridiculous ways to kill time. Public and political life so full of corruption and nepotism. She wrote articles making her *persona non grata* among the elite. She was avoided, and people whispered behind her back. She had only one friend within the class she had been born in to. She wanted to use her earned and inherited immense wealth to support projects in various ways to uplift the living conditions for the many underprivileged. The plan was that she, when she turned 75, would have in her possession only a convenient 2-bedroom apartment and a life insurance giving her a good life. For some incomprehensible reason, I was the one to make her release her flirtatious desires, her love, and her lusts.

27

As I arrived at the Växjö Public Library at ten Thursday morning, a neat little office had been prepared for me. All numbers of Växjö Daily issued between April and November 1937 were piled on the table. The Swedish sense of order is wonderful and admirable, sometimes a bit trying.

I had little time to waste, although at the same time I wanted to show thankfulness to the library staff by joining them for coffee breaks now and then. Next morning, Friday, I was booked on the train from Växjö at 8.10 to arrive at Copenhagen International Airport at 10.33, one hour before Saku's arrival. Then I simply must force this murder case out of my mind for a few days. Saku expects me to be totally focussed on her. Her wish will be fulfilled. I feel like falling to the ground melting and being dispersed into a puddle of rainwater when I close my eyes and imagine her standing in front of me. I have planned everything carefully. We will stay one night at the top floor in Scandic Hotel Triangle in Malmö with a beautiful view over the bridge, the strait between Sweden and Denmark, and the skyline of Copenhagen in the sunset, see aircrafts touch ground and take off, have dinner at Indian Haweli with my son and his girlfriend, next day take a train up to Växjö, pick up my car parked at Sivert's place, and then drive home to Hällerum which will take about two hours including a coffee break. Each minute will be so wonderful. I have asked my brother-in-law to light fires in the tiled stoves both in the living room and in our bedroom. Saku will be spoilt to an extent that no one on earth has been spoilt ever before. She will receive so many compliments that she will feel dizzy. Saku is a master at accepting compliments. When I say that her ankles and calves are the most beautiful on earth, then she reacts as if she knows what I say is true, which it is, and she shows she is ecstatically happy about this undeniable fact. No one can look as happy as Saku does at such moments.

I forced myself out of my dream world and started with Växjö Daily issued on 2nd of April 1937. This was two weeks after Lawrence Swenson got his passport stamped entering Sweden in Gothenburg. All specimen of the journal were thin, usually 8 pages. I soon realized that pages 4 and 5 always were devoted to activities in the local churches. Announcements, callings to meetings, commentaries, summaries of sermons and the like. The layout was professional. They must have had competent editors, printers and photographers, and good equipment. All texts and photos still today, after 80 years, easily legible and of excellent physical quality, and the paper still white.

I tried to read every word on the church-oriented pages, and I became properly bored. Local journalism at its extreme. I forced myself to feel respect for the passion and dutifulness that must have been driving forces in the production of this and hundreds of other small local newspapers in those days. This engagement has contributed to building our society to a viable democracy worth cherishing. Utterly few of these newspapers exist today.

After about an hour and a half's reading, I opened the paper of 24th of May. I had difficulties not dozing off, and I prepared mentally for the second coffee break. My eyes, however, got wide open when I read a calling to a meeting in 'Rottne Mission House' to be held on the 26th. Rottne is a small township 20 kilometres from Växjö. The announcement read: *Pastor Lawrence Johansson will give a testimony over 'Sin, Perdition, and the Justice of God'*. Lawrence! A highly uncommon name in Sweden. Has Lawrence Swenson made a half-hearted attempt to cover up his identity? I continued my reading in subsequent issues hoping to find a commentary to the meeting in Rottne, but in vain. Then, however, in the paper of the 16th of June was a calling to one of the major independent churches in central Växjö. The announcement read: *The Swedish-American Pastor Lawrence Johansson will preach, in good Swedish, over 'Sin, Perdition, and the Justice of God'. Pastor Johansson preached over the same theme in Rottne three weeks ago. The congregation became highly animated. Pastor Johansson also, in demanding words, reminded all those present of their responsibility to re-establish God's justice on earth where it has not been respected.*

The message from Pastor Johansson, possibly alias pastor Lawrence Swenson, had spread from the small 'Mission House' in the periphery into the centre of the region. The popping up of Lawrence Swenson in the area was not unexpected or sensational since Swenson himself had written to the souls in Minnesota that he had found likeminded in Wexiö. Could there be more in these papers? A sermon in this major independent church usually resulted in some sort of commentary and report in *Växjö Daily* a few days after it had occurred. On top of that, a visit by a highly profiled pastor from America must have been an unusual event, and it should have drawn considerable attention. Thus, I continued my search, and almost immediately was I richly rewarded. Already on the 18th of June, *Växjö Daily* contained a long commentary, covering a quarter page, and a big photo of good quality. The photo showed a group of 15 men organised around an excessively big man, built of muscle much more than of fat, with blond hair and a short beard. There is absolutely no doubt any more! This is the man Christoffer Swenson in Minnesota showed me on many photos. Christoffer's grandfather Lawrence Swenson. On the photo in *Växjö Daily* he had a black suit, white shirt, and a tie. He dominated the scene to 100% by his body posture of utmost strength, but even more so by the expression in his eyes. He radiated an enormous charisma, or was it a sort of madness? Or a combination of both, which can be so dangerous. The group of men around him were also well attired. At least three of them gave a strong militaristic impression both in body language and dress code. As if they tried to imitate the parade outfit of the Third Reich. This was 1937, and I felt like only the swastika was missing from these three. Is it just my personal disdain for this stiff style and for any far-right tendency that stimulates my fantasies?

The article described in concise, well formulated language, how Pastor Johansson had preached for two and a half hours and caught the full attention of the congregation. The big building had been filled to the last seat. The two and a half hours had felt like five minutes. Unlike Swedish pastors, Johansson had walked around in the room and spoken with a 'particularly loud and admonishing voice'. He had touched many of the men in the crowd on their head and looked them deeply into their eyes. When the pastor took short breaks to let his words sink in, a fallen needle would have sounded like a gunshot. Sin, crime, revenge, and punishment were the themes throughout. The souls of the attendees were profoundly shattered by the words, and horror-struck by becoming aware of their own sins.

I studied the photo in more detail, and after a while I felt a chill in my spine. To the far left stood a man of less than average height. Lean, but he looked energetic.

As if he prepared himself to leap forward. Well dressed in a grey suit, white shirt, and tie. Is this Edvin Karlsson? Willie Karl's and Nils Karlsson's older brother? It could be him! In the other photos I had seen of Edvin, he had worn working clothes, and he had been unshaven and more or less dirty from work in the peat moss. Here he is proper as if on his way to a banquet with the nobility. The photo legend simply explained that shown were pastor Johansson with some of the attendees. Mama had told me that Edvin had become deeply religious after the move from Kirsta. Did that transformation possibly start here in Växjö in the year of 1937? Was Lawrence Swenson Edvin's inspiration and mentor in that process?

I continued my search, interrupted by lunch at an unpretentious restaurant across the street. I had sole, bread crumbed and fried, boiled potatoes, green beans, a slice of lemon, dill, and a tasty remoulade sauce. Back in my office in the library I continued my search, and about an hour after lunch I made a new interesting finding. In the number from 3rd of October it was announced that Pastor Lawrence Johansson would participate in a meeting in the church called 'Sin and Punishment' on the 5th of October. This was the church pastor Löfgren, the day before, had pointed out as probably the most dogmatic in town at that time, attracting several far-right activists. The announcement read, *'Pastor Lawrence Johansson visited churches in our town in June, and his preaching still remains in the memory of those who attended. Since then, pastor Johansson has travelled in our country with his message. Now he is back in Växjö. The theme of his message will be 'God's Justified Punishment and Mankind's Obedience'.*

A commentary of the meeting in 'Sin and Punishment' occurred in *Växjö Daily* already two numbers later. Nearly half a page with two high-quality photos. Now all doubts are gone. One photo showed the pastor and a man a third his size, the man I saw on a photo in the morning, who I thought resembled Edvin Karlsson. The photo legend read: *'Pastor Johansson with his friend and disciple Edvin Karlsson'*. The synopsis of Pastor Johansson's message showed that he was satisfied with himself, and with life in general. He was as severe and disciplinary as at the meeting in June, but much more content. He expressed his thankfulness towards fate and towards the God-fearing accomplices he had met in the land of his ancestors. A few sentences read as follows: *Pastor Johansson praised the receptiveness of the good people he had met. He said 'When I return to my homeland, I know that the country of my forefathers is in good hands. Many who are present in this room will guard against the will of Satan. Specially I want to mention my friend Edvin Karlsson, who has been filled with desire to protect the good and the just, and who already has contributed immensely to defend the justice of God.' Edvin Karlsson was asked by pastor Johansson to stand up and receive the appreciation and blessings of the congregation. Edvin Karlsson spoke somewhat shyly that he was unworthy the words of Pastor Johansson. He said his life had gained meaningfulness, purpose, and security after he had promised God to submit to the teachings and leadership of Pastor Johansson.*

28

The evening in my hotel room in Växjö, and the train journey to Copenhagen International Airport in a silent compartment gave plenty of time for contemplation. This murder case has now come to an end. All that can be clarified has been clarified. Pastor Lawrence Swenson was filled with hatred and desire for revenge, and the costly journey to Sweden was probably not undertaken just for screaming out his agony. Evidently, he had managed to recruit Willie's brother Edvin as a confidant, and probably he had many other followers also. Edvin had become fully captured and obsessed by the teachings. As in Minnesota, Lawrence Swenson had exerted a unique ability to brainwash people, so that they would follow him obediently even into extreme deeds of evil. Most of his disciples probably had a weak self-confidence to start with, and they felt secure and protected in the realm of this man, so powerful both physically and mentally. How Swenson managed to get in touch with Edvin is an open question. Maybe he had found something in Willie and Alvina's home that had led him not only to the geographical spot, but also to Willie's brother.

We do not know, and we will never come to know, exactly what happened at the moment of the executions. However, it is now possible to construct plausible scenarios based on at least some known facts. For example, Helvig and Nils may have been diverted somewhere, one possibility being they were at work at my grandparents' farm while the gruesome executions were accomplished not much more than a kilometre away. Maybe a whole squadron of obsessed disciples, led by Lawrence Swenson and Edvin Karlsson, convinced as they were that they were called to cleanse the world from the influence of Satan, had taken Willie and Alvina by total surprise, and somehow managed to immobilise them, giving Lawrence the opportunity to deal the dastardly final blows with his axe. It is difficult to imagine anyone else was holding the axe, although nothing can ever be proven.

Those complicit had probably, at least initially, felt jubilant over having been a part of restoring God's justice. When Helvig and Nils returned to Kirsta and to the Wild Moss, Alvina and Willie had simply vanished, never again to be heard from. Helvig lost herself in disbelief, grief, longing, and eventually she lost even her sanity, and Nils became even more isolated within himself. Edvin, possibly to endure a bad conscience gradually overwhelming him as the spell from Pastor Lawrence lost its grip, sunk even deeper into delusions.

This is where I let it stand.

29

I stood in the arrival hall at Copenhagen International Airport and waited for Saku. The flight from Doha had landed, and she would come through the doors any minute. As has happened to me so often in similar situations, I couldn't get rid of the feeling that the whole thing is surreal. Is this true? How has it happened? Is Saku really on her way to me? Am I in a dream from which I may wake up at any moment? It is so utterly unlikely.

In mid-December four years earlier, I was in Colombo at the old colonial Mount Lavinia Hotel with three friends. One of the friends had invited us to The Cambridge Club's Christmas event. A choir sang English Christmas carols out in the rain, and thereafter there was a dinner in one of the elegant banquet halls. I had arrived in Colombo a week earlier on my way back home to Sweden from Tonga. Visiting Tonga had been a childhood dream that I had made come true. Now, on the evening of the Christmas party at Mount Lavinia, I would board a plane in Colombo shortly after midnight. Colombo-New Delhi-Copenhagen. A taxi to the airport was booked for 9.30. Thus, my friends and I walked up to the banquet hall before all others, and we simply sat down at a table laid for eight in the centre of the large banquet hall. We were unaware that seating plans hung on the wall at the entrance to the hall. After a few minutes I was mesmerized by the sight of a magically beautiful lady standing together with an older lady friend studying the seating plan. She stood with her back towards us, but something touched me deeply. My heart nearly came to a standstill when the two ladies came up to our table and sat down. The tall lady next to me was Saku!

Her lips were complicated with an asymmetry which I found irresistibly sensual. The right part of the upper lip fell slightly down over the lower lip, something that did not happen with the left part of the lips. This was particularly striking when the lips relaxed after a smile. The shape of the lips is most complex, and still today, after four years of acquaintance, when I close my eyes, I cannot memorize fully the form. These magical lips, the long, elegant fingers, the skin like milk chocolate, together with the tall, lean body, the so sensual ankles, influenced me profoundly as we sat at the table. We introduced ourselves by name. She listened and smiled. I am not an extrovert, I do not speak easily, and despite me being highly educated and experienced in many areas, in fact I'm a lousy conversationalist. I have much to say, but when I do speak most people struggle to understand what I mean. On top of all that, I have difficulties making myself heard in noisy places, and difficulties to hear what people tell me when others talk simultaneously. Never before had I, outside of the professional arena, met someone who so effortlessly understood what I meant, and who seemed so honestly interested in what I said. This was fully clear to me after less than a minute.

A few minutes later the rest of the dinner guests flooded into the banquet hall. Of course, my friends and I sat at the wrong table, so we had to move. I had talked to Saku for not more than 5 minutes. When I had to leave the banquet hall for my taxi, I did something completely atypical of me. I walked up to Saku, put my hand on her shoulder, and left her a piece of paper with my email address. She smiled at me, and I was affected to the extent that only with difficulties could I walk out of the room. Later she said my hand on her shoulders had sent wonderful impulses through her body. She also said she had felt a slight emptiness that I had not looked back on my way out. I told her I could not look back because then I might very well have fallen to the floor, or on top of one of the tables and created chaos in the room. I had entered a different world.

Finally, Saku came through the doors into the arrival hall. She looked around. Is it true that this supernaturally good-looking and self-confident woman is on her way to me? Who do I believe I am? An impulse told me to creep on the floor and hide behind a pillar, but I was like paralysed. Now she saw me, and she became so overwhelmingly happy. She dropped the handles of the two rollers so that they slid over the marble floor, and she ran a few steps up to me and hugged and kissed me, tears on her cheeks.

"How I have missed you! How I have longed for you!"

On the train on the bridge across the strait over to Sweden we sat tightly together. Her thigh was pressed against me, and her head rested on my shoulder.

www.ingramcontent.com/pod-product-compliance
Lightning Source LLC
Chambersburg PA
CBHW051231210726
48290CB00003B/895